# Montana
## ★ MAVERICKS™

**Stories of family and romance
beneath the Big Sky!**

**"All right, Jilly.
That kiss scared the hell out of me."**

She stepped away from the table and crossed
her arms, eyes tempting him like two Hershey's
kisses. "No one knows you like I do, Jeff. I
understand your love of flying, your need for
freedom. And even if I were crazy in love with
you, I wouldn't expect anything from you, other
than friendship."

That was good, wasn't it?

Before he could respond, she added, "I hope
you won't allow that kiss—as hot as it was—to ruin
what we have. I'd like to keep you in my life."

"I've forgotten it already," he lied. Then he gave
her a hug to prove he wasn't going to let the kiss
affect him.

Trouble was, it already had.

Far more than he was willing to admit.

# JUDY DUARTE

*Big Sky Baby*

Published by Silhouette Books

**America's Publisher of Contemporary Romance**

Special thanks and acknowledgment to Judy Duarte
for her contribution to the Montana Mavericks series.

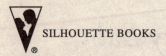 **SILHOUETTE BOOKS**

ISBN-13: 978-0-373-36242-4

Recycling programs
for this product may
not exist in your area.

BIG SKY BABY

Copyright © 2003 by Harlequin Books S.A.

## JUDY DUARTE

always knew there was a book inside her, but since English was her least-favorite subject in school, she never considered herself a writer. An avid reader who enjoys a happy ending, Judy couldn't shake the dream of creating a book of her own.

Her dream became a reality in March of 2002, when Silhouette Special Edition released her first book, *Cowboy Courage*. Since then, she has published more than twenty novels. Her stories have touched the hearts of readers around the world. And in July of 2005, Judy won the prestigious Readers' Choice Award for *The Rich Man's Son*.

Judy makes her home near the beach in Southern California. When she's not cooped up in her writing cave, she's spending time with her somewhat enormous but delightfully close family.

To Don Ham and Duke Dunn,
my pilot connections. You have no idea how
much I appreciate the time you spent with me,
answering questions, offering technical advice
and looking over scenes.

And to Joe Trapp, whose wife, Jessica,
thrust a phone in his hand and said,
"Honey, talk to my friend."
Thank you from the bottom of my heart.
This book is for you.

# *Chapter One*

Jeff Forsythe was back in town.

All right, Jilly Davis thought, maybe temporarily, but he was home just the same. And it was a darn good thing, because she could really use a friend in the flesh right now, not to mention a hug.

When Jeff left to join the forestry service five years ago, Jilly had felt somewhat abandoned. But unlike every other male she'd known, he'd called her every week, insisting on maintaining their friendship.

Jilly scanned the green, woodsy interior of the florist shop Jeff had loaned her the money to buy. She hoped he liked what she'd done to the place, especially the window display that changed every couple of days.

She'd gotten a deal on Gerber daisies this week, and using pots of the pastel-hued flowers and a quaint cast-iron bench, she'd created a parklike setting to catch the eyes of the locals who passed by.

Jeff had always said she was artistic, and apparently he'd been right. Jilly's Lilies was a blooming success.

Imagine that. The scruffy little Davis girl from the wrong side of the tracks was now a genuine member of the Rumor Chamber of Commerce—and a homeowner to boot. That was quite a feat for someone like her to accomplish, especially at the ripe old age of twenty-three.

Who would have guessed?

No one but Jeff Forsythe, that's for sure.

What made their mismatched friendship even more surprising was the fact that he'd been born with the proverbial silver spoon in his mouth.

Jeff often referred to himself as a shirttail relative of the MonMart Kingsleys, but the shirttail had been made of the finest imported silk.

His socialite mother had been Carolyn Kingsley's younger sister, and when she died in a fiery car accident, six-year-old Jeff was sent to live with his aunt and uncle on the Kingsley ranch.

Jeff was a very wealthy man by virtue of his mother's money alone. The Kingsley riches only added to his considerable worth. But you'd never know it by looking at him. Jeff was one of the most unassuming guys Jilly had ever met.

More times than she could count, Jeff had ventured over to her run-down, trashy side of the tracks, something that had caused his wealthy, straitlaced Aunt Carolyn a great deal of worry. Still, the social icon of Rumor hadn't been able to discourage their friendship. Nor had the passing of time.

Jilly hadn't seen Jeff in five years, but she doubted he'd changed much. Tall, lanky. Dark hair, nice, but serious smile. He was the one constant force in her life.

And her very best friend.

She'd missed him something fierce when he left town, but their friendship continued to flourish over the telephone and through a jillion e-mails.

Who needed Dear Abby when a girl had her very own Jeff Forsythe to keep her in line, to listen to her problems, to encourage her hopes and dreams?

Jilly had a penchant for getting herself into one jam or another, and Jeff's friendship had proven to be an invaluable asset. She had a feeling he actually liked coming to her rescue, although he probably wouldn't admit it. Either way, the years had only deepened their relationship.

Each time the bell on the florist shop door rang, she glanced up from her work, hoping to see her old friend. At a quarter to five the bell chimed again, and this time her glance was rewarded.

Only it wasn't the gangly kid she remembered who stood in the doorway of her shop. It was a tall, dark-haired god of epic proportions—a sight worthy of a gasp, a second glance or an all-out gaping stare.

Lanky Jeff Forsythe had filled out, grown up and

aged to perfection. When he removed his aviator glasses, eyes the color of the Montana sky locked on hers, piercing her heart and sending a swarm of bewildered butterflies to her tummy.

If Jeff hadn't grown used to feminine appreciation, he'd better.

His smile broadened, revealing a set of dashing dimples. "Hey, good-lookin'. Where can I find the owner of this establishment?"

"You found her, flyboy." Jilly hoped he hadn't seen or sensed her reaction to the sight of him.

Sheesh. Talk about buff and good-looking. If he weren't her best friend, she might find herself gawking at him. Heck, she *was* gawking at him.

Get a grip, Jilly told herself. It's only Jeff.

"I hope you stopped by to give me a hug," she said, trying desperately to thwart a runaway sexual attraction to her friend.

That's right. *Her friend.*

"It's good to see you, Jilly." His deep voice settled around her, cloaking her in crushed velvet and causing her heart to slip a gear before jetting into overdrive.

She dropped a sprig of greenery on the table and dashed into his arms, eager to feel his familiar embrace.

He lifted her from the floor as though she were merely a rag doll, and a musky, woodsy scent accosted her. She struggled to act nonchalant, unaffected by his touch.

Who was this gorgeous guy? And what had he done with her best friend?

"I missed you," she said, although she hadn't realized how much until he'd walked in the door. "Maybe I should hang on tight so you can't get away."

Jeff held Jilly close, savoring the earthy scent of flowers and spice. It had been too damn long since he'd seen the little brown-haired girl with the chipped-tooth smile.

He'd missed her, too.

When he left Rumor five years ago, he had no intention of coming back, other than for visits. It wasn't that he didn't care about his family and friends, but he'd been born with a case of wanderlust and an intrinsic love of flying. By the time he was sixteen, when he'd taken control of his very first plane, a yellow Piper Cub, his course had been set.

"It's good to have you home," she said.

"I'm not home. Not really."

They both knew it was the fire that began near Rumor and continued to rage in the Custer National Forest that had called him back to town indefinitely.

As part of the Modular Airborne Firefighting System, or MAFFS, Jeff had been ordered to report to the fire command center before dawn tomorrow, but he made time for a quick detour by Jilly's Lilies to see his old friend.

God, he'd missed her. Missed her smile, her happy

laugh. Missed the tales of her adventures or—more often than not—her misadventures.

Looking out for her had been a job he'd accepted a long time ago, and after five years of hearing her voice and reading her e-mails, he enjoyed holding her close.

In fact, he was enjoying it *way* too much.

Before she pummeled his back with her fist, begged to be put down and asked if he'd gone stark-raving nuts, Jeff released his hold and set her feet upon the floor.

He hoped she didn't suspect he'd found the hug far more stimulating than was appropriate, but for some reason she felt good in his arms. Damn good.

As Jilly stood before him, wearing a plain white T-shirt and jeans—nothing fancy—he couldn't help but stare. She wasn't the same skinny kid he'd remembered. She'd grown up and filled out in an alluring, womanly way.

Her brown eyes glimmered like a pool of melted chocolate, drawing him deep into her gaze. He seemed to flounder there for a while.

"What's the matter?" she asked.

Hell, he didn't really know. Or maybe he did and wasn't ready to face the truth. "You've changed."

"So have you." Her mouth quirked into a silly grin, but he couldn't seem to find any humor in the bodily reaction that stirred his hormones and heated his blood.

The girl he remembered was gone, replaced by a

woman with an earthy sex appeal he'd never noticed. No wonder Cain Kincaid—the horn dog of the fire department—had chased after her, nose sniffing and tail wagging.

Jilly batted his arm. "What's the matter?"

"Nothing." It wasn't exactly a lie. Something was the matter, but he wasn't sure what.

Had her breasts always been that…full? Or maybe it was just the form-fitting shirt she wore. His gaze traveled down to the jeans that hugged her hips, then he caught himself.

For cripe's sake, Jilly was his best friend, not some woman he was trying to hit on.

She brushed a hand across her cheek, pushing aside a silky strand of honey-brown hair, and smiled at him in a shy sort of way.

He supposed she was feeling a bit awkward, like he was, which was odd. They'd always been comfortable with each other, like a brother and sister who enjoyed being together, in spite of occasional squabbles.

"Are you hungry?"

Chocolate-brown eyes. Honey-colored hair. His appetite had been stirred, that was for sure, but she was talking about food. "I hadn't thought about it, but I suppose so. What do you have in mind?"

"I put a roast in the Crock-Pot at home. If you give me a minute to lock up, we can go to my place and catch up on things."

His aunt and uncle would probably shoot him if

they found out he'd stopped by Jilly's before going out to the ranch. Of course, they'd given up on lecturing him ages ago, after that visit to the shrink in Billings.

Jeff couldn't remember the good doctor's name, but the guy had told his aunt to ease up on him. And she had, especially where Jilly was concerned.

"A home-cooked meal sounds good," Jeff said. "Besides, I'd like to see your house."

"I thought you would." Jilly offered him a smile, then grabbed his hand and gave it a squeeze, sending a burst of heat pulsing through his blood. "Come on. Let's get out of here."

Yeah. Let's.

They took separate cars, since Jeff couldn't stay long. But he was looking forward to seeing the little house on Lost Lane he'd encouraged her to buy. It was a fixer-upper in the better part of town, and Jeff had known it would increase in value with a little paint, some elbow grease and Jilly's artistic knack.

Jilly arrived first, opened the door, then dashed inside, while Jeff lagged behind.

The faint scent of ash and smoke laced the air, reminding him of the destruction the fire had ravished on the forestlands outside of town, the job he had to do tomorrow. He'd often flown out with MAFFS, fighting a number of devastating blazes, but he had a personal stake in this one, since it was so close to Rumor.

He'd no more than stepped into a spacious living room that needed more furniture, when a bark sounded and a scruffy blur raced into view like a miniature tornado.

"Look, Posey. We've got company." Jilly stooped to pick up the small, scruffy dog. Well, it sounded like a dog, but it looked more like an automated dust mop minus the stick.

Jeff laughed. "Where did you find that thing?"

"That thing?" She lifted a brow and frowned. "You'll hurt her feelings. This is Posey, the best friend I've got. Other than you, of course."

The ugly little dust mop wiggled in her arms, licking her face.

She always did like strays—dogs, cats, a guy like Cain Kincaid, whose sole purpose in life was to jump the bones of every woman in the county.

"What do you think?" she asked.

About what? The fact she'd finally listened to his repeated advice and dumped Cain a couple of months ago?

"I've still got a lot to do, but the house is coming together."

Jeff scanned the mint-green living room, noting the faint smell of fresh paint. She'd decorated the windows with lacy curtains he suspected were handmade.

A floral sofa and a beige easy chair completed the sparse furnishings, but he figured she could pick up additional furniture later, one piece at a time.

He shot her an appreciative smile. "It looks good, Jilly."

Having a real home had always been a dream of hers, and he was glad he'd had a small hand in helping her buy her own place. "Now all you need is the porch swing and that little picket fence you've always talked about."

"Thanks." She put the squirmy dust mop on the floor, then offered him that chipped-tooth smile he found so endearing. It was, after all, her badge of courage.

On Jeff's first day at Rumor Elementary, Cain Kincaid had taunted him for being the new kid in their first-grade class. Things might not have escalated, had the school bully, along with a third-grade crony, joined in, cornering Jeff behind the handball court.

Only six years old, and clearly outnumbered, Jeff had doubled up his fists, ready to defend himself to the death. But from out of the blue, a scrawny, brown-haired girl came to his rescue, butting the bully from the side and sending them all flying toward the concrete backboard. Thank goodness a teacher intervened, but not before Jilly earned her battle scar—a chipped front tooth. From then on, each time she smiled, Jeff was reminded of her bravery.

They became friends that day, and their friendship had endured through the years.

"It's good to have you back," she said.

"Yeah, well, under the circumstances, I'm not

really back. Once that fire is contained, I'll be gone."

"You're here now." She flashed him a smile. "Let's enjoy our time together."

He intended to, even though things had grown a bit weird between them.

Since they'd been apart and since she'd revealed a few details about her relationship with Cain, Jeff had started to feel something, although he wasn't sure what.

At times it seemed a lot like jealousy. He shrugged it off, though, determined not to consider the possibility of romance—temporary or otherwise. Jilly needed someone who would make a home with her in Rumor, someone who wasn't a freedom-loving pilot married to his job.

Besides, Jeff lived in Colorado, close to his MAFFS outfit. He thrived on being on call, on taking off at a moment's notice. And he loved the excitement, the danger.

There couldn't possibly be a fate worse than being grounded in Rumor for good, pushing a lawn mower and living vicariously by television on Saturday nights.

Jeff was a free spirit. And he had no intention of having his wings clipped—by anyone.

An hour later Jilly and Jeff sat at the scarred oak dining room table she'd picked up at the thrift store in Whitehorn. A vase of yesterday's tulips and white tapered candles in brass candlesticks graced the worn but clean linen tablecloth.

She would have offered him a glass of wine, but knew he was a real stickler for flight regulations and safety. So she didn't bother to ask and gave him iced tea instead.

They dined on roast beef, red potatoes and baby carrots. All the while, Posey sat near the table, waiting patiently for someone to have pity and toss her a treat. Strange as it may sound, Jilly understood how the little mutt felt.

As a kid, she'd often waited for a scrap of affection, a kind word, a warm smile.

Of course, things had changed once her mother died and Jilly moved out of the run-down house she'd grown up in.

"Aren't you going to put that dog outside?" Jeff asked.

"Nope." She tossed her two-legged friend a crooked smile. "Posey lives indoors."

Jeff merely shook his head and went back to eating. When he wasn't looking, she slipped her furry pal a chunk of meat.

Both her friends seemed pleased with the taste of her culinary efforts and chomped away. She wished she could take more credit for the meal, but she'd merely dumped everything in a Crock-Pot this morning and let the handy-dandy appliance do the rest.

Jilly picked at her food. Although hungry, she

was struggling with a diet that wasn't working. She'd gained weight lately.

As Jeff buttered a piece of bread, she discreetly unsnapped her jeans to give her waistline some relief. It seemed that most of her weight had settled in the stomach, bloating her tummy. Her energy level had dipped, big-time, causing her to want a midday nap.

And a few other things had been bothering her, too, like a nervous stomach that seemed to be much worse than ever before. Of course, she blamed that on her recent breakup with Cain, but just to be on the safe side, she'd scheduled an appointment at the Rumor Family Clinic on Monday afternoon.

Chances were her weird complaints were nothing but residual stress caused by that lousy relationship she'd finally ended.

When would she learn how to sort through men and choose one worth keeping?

Jeff looked up from his meal. "This is really good, Jilly. You've become a great cook."

"Thanks."

When she glanced up and caught him looking at her with those big-sky eyes, something passed between them, and the air grew heavy, laden with unspoken words and thoughts.

Jilly didn't know what was tumbling around in Jeff's mind, but she suspected it was some of the same confusion that plagued her. The friendship she'd come to depend upon had changed.

She and Jeff had shared a lot of meals in the past—pizza, a burger and fries. But boy, oh, boy, things were different this time. Much different.

Maybe they were both a little uneasy with their new…their new what?

Awareness?

Attraction?

Darned if she knew what was happening, but this whole surreal evening reminded her of the movie, *When Harry Met Sally.*

Was this what Harry meant when he said men and women couldn't be friends because sex got in the way?

Well, she wasn't about to let awkwardness rain on their reunion. Friendships like the one they shared came along once in a lifetime, and she wasn't going to risk losing the one-and-only stable element in her life.

Jeff pushed his chair from the table and slowly stood, breaking the tension that hovered around them. "I'd better go. I've got an early day tomorrow."

Jilly nodded. "I understand."

"But I'll help you with the dishes."

"Don't bother," Jilly said, fighting a grin. "Posey will help me clean up."

Jeff furrowed his brow and studied her as though he suspected she planned to let the dog lick the plates clean.

The naughty side of her wanted to let him believe she was serious, but her conscience wouldn't let her tease him tonight. Not when he had to fly out tomorrow morning and fight that fire. The danger of his job was never far from her mind.

"I'm joking, flyboy. Posey just keeps me company."

He grabbed her by the hand and drew her to his side. "I can take a joke as well as the next guy, but I never know what you'll come up with next."

She laughed. "Well, if you're leaving, you'd better give me a hug."

"I've always got a hug for my best friend." He pulled her close, sending her pulse racing and her imagination soaring. And when he brushed a goodbye kiss across her cheek, her breath caught and her heart spun like a little toy top with nowhere to move.

The men in her life had always let her down, but not Jeff Forsythe, the best friend she'd ever had.

Yet, in spite of herself, she had begun to look at Jeff in a new and sensual light.

And it left her terribly uneasy.

Especially when she knew her best friend had no intention of putting down roots in Rumor.

# Chapter Two

Jilly sat in the waiting room at the Rumor Family Clinic, listening for her name to be called.

The wind had shifted that afternoon, taking the scent of smoke and the haze of ash with it and giving the Rumor community another respite from the fire that continued to blaze and darken the southern sky. It seemed a waste of time to be indoors on a day like this.

Afternoon sunlight poured into the room through two huge bay windows, casting a bright and cheerful glow on all who waited patiently, yet Jilly felt tense and fidgety.

She glanced at her watch—4:08 p.m.

Hopefully, they'd get her in and out so she could go back to work. She'd purposely scheduled the time so Blake Cameron, the teenager she'd hired as part-time help, could watch the florist shop for her.

She glanced at her watch again—4:09 p.m. Maybe she should cancel the appointment and head back to work, but she was hoping Dr. Holmes could tell her those weird symptoms she'd been having and those strange sensations she'd been feeling were all in her head.

The door to the back offices opened, and a dark-haired, matronly nurse held a file close to her chest and stood in the doorway. "Jilly Davis?"

Too late to cancel now, she supposed. After placing the magazine she'd been reading on the table, she stood and followed the nurse down the hall that led to the examining rooms.

"Will you step on the scale, please?"

"Sure. Mind if I slip off my shoes first?" she asked. Maybe take off my watch and my ring, shave my legs?

Sheesh. Jilly knew her weight was up. She couldn't button her pants anymore and even her bras were snug. She'd tried to diet, but every time she turned around, she had the nervous munchies. She'd blamed her food cravings on stress, following her breakup with Cain.

"Not too bad," the heavyset nurse said. "Only five pounds up from last winter, when you came in for your yearly pap smear."

"Five pounds a year can add up," Jilly said. "I'm not happy about the weight gain, since most of it's in my torso. I'm feeling a lot like Humpty-Dumpty."

The nurse smiled. "I know what you mean."

Jilly supposed the plump woman did. As she was led to the small examining room, she did a little math.

*Wow.* If she gained five pounds a year, by the time she was thirty-three, she'd be fifty pounds overweight. This eating spree had to stop.

When they reached exam room three, Jilly expected to have to strip down and put on the stupid gown that opened down the back. Fortunately, she wasn't asked to undress.

As she sat on the edge of the paper-lined examining table, the nurse took her blood pressure. At least *that* wasn't up.

While the woman made notes on the chart, Jilly unhooked the button on her pants and rubbed the reddened indenture the waistband had made. Gosh, she hoped it wasn't a tumor or something like that. Maybe she was just getting fat and sassy and needed to take up jogging.

"Dr. Holmes will be right with you," the woman said, leaving Jilly to wait in the stark room and worry about her health.

Fortunately, she didn't have to wait long. Dr. Holmes, a tall, pretty woman with golden-brown hair entered the exam room, holding Jilly's chart. "Good afternoon. What seems to be the trouble?"

"It's probably nothing," Jilly said, "but I've been feeling kind of weird lately."

"How so?" the doctor asked.

"I've been tired. And I've gained weight. My

breasts have been swollen and tender, although they're feeling better now. A while back, I had some intestinal flu symptoms. At the time, I didn't worry much about it because I tend to get a nervous stomach, and I'd been going through a stressful period back then." Jilly shrugged. "Like I said, it's probably nothing."

"When was your last period?"

Huh? Her last period? Well, she wasn't really sure. She tried to conjure a mental calendar to no avail.

"About a month ago, I think. It was pretty light." She looked at the doctor, hoping the woman would understand why she had never bothered to count the days. "My periods are really irregular. Sometimes they're kind of light and scanty, other times heavy. I guess I should keep better track of them, but since they're so hard to predict, it doesn't seem to matter."

"Could you be pregnant?"

"Pregnant?" Jilly nearly fell off the examining table. "I don't think so."

She and Cain had broken up two months ago. And they'd always used condoms. In fact, she'd been so careful and obsessive about contraception that she couldn't possibly be pregnant.

Just the thought of being an unwed mother scared the willies out of her.

Not that she didn't want a baby, but she had her life on track right now, and she was aiming toward pillar-of-the-community status. Having a baby out of wedlock would set her back big-time—back to the Davis family values she'd tried hard to break free of and surpass.

"It's possible to be pregnant and still have a scanty period," Dr. Holmes said. "I'll step out of the room while you undress. Then, after I examine you, I'll have a better idea of what's going on."

A few minutes later Jilly lay on the small table, her feet in the stirrups and her head spinning wildly. *I can't be pregnant. I just can't.*

Stress altered menstrual cycles, too, she reminded herself. And Cain had certainly caused her a ton of stress. This all seemed to be his fault.

Of course, it was her fault, too.

Why couldn't she be attracted to a decent guy, one who could make a commitment and be a family man?

"Well," Dr. Holmes said, letting out a soft sigh and smiling. "You're definitely pregnant. About four months, according to my estimate. I'm going to order some lab work, and an ultrasound."

Four months pregnant? It was nearly too much for Jilly to take in.

But she could add. And that meant in five months she was going to be a mother.

An unwed mother.

Her heart sank. There went all her plans and dreams. She wanted nothing more than to be a wife and mother, to have the respectability her parents hadn't been able to provide her. But that plan required marriage first, then a baby.

Again, she had the overwhelming urge to lash out and blame a certain good-looking fireman. Her life had been all nice and tidy until sweet-talkin' Cain came sauntering into her shop and turned her world upside down. And now she was having his baby.

She doubted he'd be happy to hear the news, especially since he'd made it clear that he didn't particularly like kids. The whole darn mess seemed to crash down upon her, until she came up with an option she hadn't realized she had.

Maybe Cain didn't need to know about the baby.

She could keep the paternity of her baby a secret, and if Cain suspected the child was his, he wouldn't utter a word. Not if it meant he'd be liable for child support. A footloose guy like that didn't want any strings to tie him down. Or so he'd made it clear the one time she'd pressed him for a commitment.

"I'm not the marrying kind, babe," Cain had said.

Well, that was fine with her. Jilly couldn't imagine being married to a lying womanizer like him.

She glanced at Dr. Holmes, wondering if she had any advice or a magical potion to make Jilly's life fall into place.

"I'd like you to start taking prenatal vitamins." The doctor pulled a notepad out of the pocket of her lab coat and began to write. "I'll jot down the name of the brand I'd prefer you buy. The sooner you start taking them the better."

"All right," Jilly said, taking the sheet of paper the doctor handed her. She was glad to have a note, something in writing, otherwise, she might forget the brand altogether.

"Do you have any questions or concerns?"

Questions or concerns? Heck, she had a ton of them, but they slipped around inside her head like the spinning fruit and numbers on a slot machine, and she had no idea which question would pop out first.

"I'm scared, Dr. Holmes. And confused. I don't even know…" Tears welled up in her eyes, and her tongue turned to mush.

The doctor snatched a tissue from the countertop, handed it to Jilly and slipped an arm around her shoulder. "Why don't you make an appointment to come back in and see me later this week, when you've had a chance to think about things. We can talk about options."

"Options?"

"Well, you don't have to keep the baby."

Give her baby up?

No way.

Jilly didn't need to hear any options. Her pregnancy might be totally unplanned, but this was her baby. It wasn't the poor kid's fault its mommy made a big mistake in the daddy-picking process.

"I don't need to think about options, Doctor, but I would like to talk to you about…stuff." Jilly swiped the tissue under her eyes. It was times like this that she really missed having a mother, although she hadn't been able to depend upon her mom when she'd been alive. But the fact was, Jilly didn't have anyone, not a sister or even a real girlfriend—the kind that kept secrets and didn't blab them all over town. "I don't have a clue what to expect. And I'm nervous."

"I can understand that." Dr. Holmes smiled. "I'll have to check the schedule, but I think Friday afternoon is open."

"Thanks," Jilly muttered.

"Do you have someone you can talk to? A mother or sister? A friend?"

"Yeah, sort of." She had a friend, all right. Only this had to be the heaviest problem she'd ever dumped on him.

"Feel free to call me anytime," the doctor said.

"Don't worry, I'll be okay."

Now all Jilly needed to do was convince herself that she could handle this unplanned turn of events.

Jilly carried her secret for two days before she gave in to the urge to contact Jeff.

Who else could she turn to? Certainly not Cain. Jeff had always been there for her, even when he and MAFFS were out fighting fires. She figured e-mail would be her best bet, especially if she tried to reach him through his business address.

Her only other resort was to call Reed Kingsley,

Jeff's cousin. But Reed was the Rumor fire chief and Cain's boss.

Quite frankly, she didn't want to go that route.

In the past, Jeff had always managed to answer her e-mail. Eventually.

*Hey, flyboy,* she typed into the computer screen. He'd earned the nickname by dragging her out to every airport in the county to look at planes and talk to the air junkies who hung out there. *Can you give me a call when you get a chance? I need to talk to you.*

It was another day and evening before Jeff read her e-mail and got a chance to use his cell phone.

"What's up, Jilly?"

When she heard his voice over the line, for the first time in her life, she found it hard to speak. She carried the portable phone to the sofa and plopped down.

Posey, having followed her around for days and sensing her distress, hopped up to join her.

"Are you there?" Jeff asked.

Yeah, she was here. Pregnant and struggling with how to form the words. She cleared her voice and forced herself to speak. "I need a friend."

The simple phrase had become a code between them, letting him know she'd screwed something up in her life and needed him to bail her out.

And she'd certainly "screwed things up" this time. She rolled her eyes at the apt description.

"Jilly, I'm a bit tied up right now, but I'll do what I can. What's wrong?"

She squeezed the receiver until her knuckles ached. How could she tell Jeff that she was pregnant by the guy he'd repeatedly warned her about? The guy he'd never liked since grade school. The guy she should have known to avoid from day one.

Well, she certainly couldn't keep Jeff hanging on the line, not when he was probably calling from the command post at the fire.

"I'm pregnant."

"You're what?" Static crackled on the line, but she had a feeling he would have voiced the same question had he been standing next to her.

*I'm what?* had been her initial reaction, too. It still was. Lord, would she ever get used to the idea of being pregnant?

She blew out a weary sigh. "I really don't know how it happened, or how I failed to notice the signs. But I'm four months pregnant, Jeff."

The line froze, or so it seemed. Not even the static responded, which led her to wonder if he'd hung up. She shook off the old insecurity. Jeff wouldn't do that to her.

"Have you told Cain?"

Heck no, she hadn't called that jerk. What did Cain have to offer her? More lies? More stress?

She needed a friend, someone she could depend on. She needed Jeff, like she never had before.

Jilly had never been one to wade into deep

psychological waters, but Jeff was a stabilizing force in her life, and his sobering influence curtailed the rebellious streak that often got her into trouble.

And she was in big trouble now.

"I'm not going to tell Cain anything," she said. "Even if he was inclined to offer marriage or a hand in child rearing, I've learned my lesson. He's not daddy or husband material. I'm going to go through this alone."

"Now, just a minute. That guy has a responsibility to live up to, even if it's just sending you a monthly check for child support."

"I don't need him or his money." Jilly was used to living on a budget and depending upon herself.

"You need his financial support. And he needs to face up to his responsibilities—for once in his life."

Jeff was probably right. He always was, so it seemed. What would she have done without him?

When he left town five years ago, she was sure he was leaving her, like every other male she'd ever known. But he'd called her every week, insisting on maintaining a friendship. And she was glad he had, although their friendship did have a downside.

Jeff often took on the role of a big brother and criticized everyone she'd ever dated, saying the guy wasn't good enough for her, which was sweet, she supposed.

It was also true, unfortunately.

Jilly never picked the right kind of guy. Her recent experience with Cain was certainly proof of that.

But Jeff was right, as much as she hated to admit it. She had to tell Cain about the baby, even though she didn't want to.

Jilly had always dreamed of falling in love, getting married and having a baby—in that order. Guilt assaulted her, and she hated the idea of parenting a child with a man who wasn't the white knight she'd once thought.

But worse, she dreaded raising a child in a single-parent home.

Usually able to don a tough exterior, she broke down in blubbery tears.

Jeff couldn't stand to hear Jilly cry. She was such a tough cookie on the outside, but inside she was delicate, a tenderhearted softy.

He gave her time to cry, which is what he would have done had he been there to hold her. Still, her tears always did a number on him, and he needed time to think things through, plan his words of support.

Her call had taken him aback, not just because he was busy at the makeshift fire-fighting headquarters, but because he hadn't liked Cain in the first place.

He supposed he could understand her attraction to the cocky fireman. Jilly had never been entirely convinced that she amounted to much—a result of her mother's criticism and the community gossip, he'd always suspected. No wonder she'd fallen for a line of bull when good-looking, fast-talking Cain paid attention to her.

Jeff suddenly felt an overwhelming compulsion to slam a fist into the macho fireman's face.

Maybe he was jealous of the guy, in a strange sort of way. The guy who married Jilly was going to be a hell of a lucky man. And Jeff hated to think that man would be Cain.

"Are you okay?" he asked, when he figured Jilly had gotten her tears and sobs under control.

She sniffled. "Yes. I guess so. Don't worry about me. I'll be all right."

Yeah, that's what she always told him when she got into trouble. But this was different. More serious. She was pregnant, for cripe's sake.

"I know it'll be tough for you to do, but you've got to tell him about the baby, honey."

The term of endearment had slipped out, through no intention of his own. But it felt right. Jilly was a sweetheart, and she didn't deserve any of the crap Cain had dealt her.

"Okay," she said, her voice shaking and laced with tears she would probably continue to shed long after they hung up the phone. It killed him to see her brokenhearted, worried, alone.

"I'll tell him tomorrow," she said.

"It's the right thing to do, Jilly."

She blew out a sigh. "I guess that's why I called you. I knew you'd see things more clearly than me. And maybe Cain will react differently than I expect."

Jeff doubted Cain would be man enough to step

up to the plate and do right by her and the baby, but she owed him the truth.

Again Jeff was struck with the urge to batter Cain senseless, but that wouldn't help Jilly.

Jeff had been looking after her for years and would continue to do so. That's what friends were for. "I'll stop by and see you as soon as we get this fire under control."

She sniffled. "I'd like that."

"You'll make a good mom, Jilly."

"Thanks."

"Listen, honey—" Oops, the endearment slipped out again, but he continued anyway, desperately wanting to say something sensible and helpful "—everything is going to work out fine. Just wait and see."

Somehow Jeff would make sure of it.

When Jilly hung up the telephone, she stroked the little dog that had curled up on her lap.

"What do you think, Posey?"

The mutt stood up and licked her chin.

"What would I do without you or Jeff?"

Posey whimpered, then gave a little bark.

Jilly glanced at the phone, wishing she had the kind of news that didn't need to be delivered to Cain in person.

What a coward.

Still, she didn't want to show up on his doorstep and find he was on duty at the fire station.

What the heck. Why not call and see if he answered? She could always hang up.

And that's what she decided to do. Fortunately, she got his answering machine. "I'm out and about. Leave a message and I'll call you when I feel like it."

Most people found his recording humorous. But they didn't know him like Jilly did. The fact was Cain only called a person back when he felt like it.

How many times had she waited for a return call? How many times had she wondered where he was and why he was late?

She thought about the last time she'd seen him. He'd been out with another fireman, a buddy, he'd said. But a telltale smear of fire-engine-red lipstick on his collar suggested otherwise.

"While ol' Frank and I were tossing down a few brews at Joe's bar, the waitress slipped on a lemon wedge someone had dropped on the floor. I caught her, just before she fell." He'd winked at Jilly, then added, "Once a hero, always a hero."

That poor waitress must have fallen hard, because Cain bore a small bruise on his neck. The fact that it looked suspiciously like a love bite didn't do his questionable credibility any good.

What an idiot she'd been, a definite slow learner in the relationship department.

Like the sand in an hourglass, Jeff's friendly advice finally began to sink in. The good-looking fireman had been taking her for a ride, stringing her along. Playing tetherball with her heart.

Cain had never been there when she needed him. And she really didn't expect him to do things any differently now.

But Jeff was right. He deserved to know about the baby.

She hung up the phone and sighed. Chances were Cain was on duty and at the station tonight. That meant he would be home tomorrow morning. Like it or not, it was best she got this over with.

Jilly would be on Cain's front porch after he got home from work and before he could leave.

Then she would lay her pride on the line.

## Chapter Three

Jilly parked her ten-year-old, white Ford Taurus along the curb in front of Cain's apartment building and struggled to find the courage to face him.

What would she say?

Telling a man he was going to be a father, that they were going to be parents, should be an exciting and happy time. So why did she feel as though she were stepping onto the long green mile?

Because a relationship with Cain—even one in which they only shared a child—seemed like a death sentence. Things hadn't ended well, and she'd made it clear in both tone and volume that she'd rather die than see or talk to him again.

She glanced into the rearview mirror and, catching a glimpse of the dark circles under her eyes that revealed she hadn't slept worth a darn last night, blew out a ragged sigh. She'd best get this over with.

Cain's living-room blinds were open, indicating he was indeed home. But she couldn't see inside. Had he seen her pull up?

She could still turn the Taurus around and drive away. Go home with her secret and pride in tact. It certainly felt like the right thing to do. But instead, with Jeff's advice ringing in her ears, she jerked open the car door and slipped from her vehicle.

Another wave of apprehension assaulted her. What was she doing here? Their relationship was over, and she'd never wanted to see Cain again. Of course, small-town life made completely avoiding him impossible. But this was different. Jilly was actually seeking him out and providing information that would complicate things.

She trudged up the walk, the leather soles of her sandals crunching upon the dirty concrete in a cadence that woke the coward that lived deep in her soul—the yellow-bellied weakling she'd banished years ago by playing tough guy.

*It's not too late,* the coward reminded her. *You can still turn around.*

But Jeff's voice kicked in, strong and true. *I know it'll be tough for you to do, but you've got to tell him about the baby, honey.*

Yeah. Telling Cain was the right thing to do, she supposed. Leave it to Jeff to set her on the straight-and-narrow path.

Jilly stepped around a worn leather baseball mitt someone had left on the walkway and continued up the stairs to Cain's second-level apartment. She rang the bell and wiped her palms on the sides of her jeans.

When Cain swung open the door, surprise registered briefly on his face, then he flashed her a pearly white smile. "Look who's here. A while back, you seemed pretty serious about never seeing me again, babe. Change your mind?"

She wanted to slap the smirk from his face, but crossed her arms instead. "I need to talk to you."

"Sure," he said, stepping aside. "But I've only got a few minutes. I just got a call from Reed down at the station. The wind changed, and some of us are being sent in to help fight the fire again. We're heading out in less than an hour."

Jilly nodded, then made her way into the classic bachelor's pad—leather sofa, fully stocked bar, state-of-the-art stereo system, surround sound. A dimmer switch on all the lights.

Like Jeff had said during one of their telephone conversations when she told him about how nice Cain's place was, "That's quite an impressive setup in a rented apartment. He's a player, Jilly. Watch out."

Jilly had clicked her tongue and waved him off. "Give the guy a break, will you? He's not the same kid you remember from school. He's a fireman for goodness' sake."

But Jeff had been right—as usual. Why hadn't she figured it out sooner? Before her life came tumbling down around her.

"Did you come to apologize?" Cain asked.

Of all the…

Her earlier apprehension and case of nerves flew by the wayside as righteous indignation took their place. "For what? For trusting you? For thinking you could commit to one woman for the duration of a four-month relationship?"

He shook his head and shot her a wry grin. "If you think long and hard, you'll realize I never made you any promises, babe."

She had to admit he hadn't, not really. And she tried to remember how sweet he'd been in the early part of their relationship, how he'd poured her a glass of wine, turned on the soft sound of jazz, sat her on a bar stool that faced the kitchen so she could watch him prepare a romantic dinner for two.

He was an incredible cook—much better than she was—and she'd looked forward to each meal they shared. And on those nights they hadn't spent together, he'd called her to say good-night.

But it had all been an act, a facade. He hadn't cared about her, not in the right way.

"Listen, Cain, I'll make this quick, but I can't make it easy. I'm pregnant."

His dark brow furrowed momentarily, then a slow smile broadened. "Who's the lucky guy?"

"I'm four months pregnant," she said, assuming he would count and figure it out.

He crossed his arms, the lighthearted smile turning dry. "Like I said, who's the lucky guy?"

As though having a mind of its own, her hand lashed out and slapped his face. The sound reverberated in the room, and the contact stung her palm.

He rubbed a reddened cheek. "I hope you're not going to try and blame a pregnancy on me. If you'll remember, we always used condoms. I'm not the kind of guy to take stupid chances."

Tears welled up in Jilly's eyes. "I wasn't even going to tell you about it."

"Then why did you?" Cain leaned against the armrest of the sofa. "I'm not the marrying kind, Jilly. And I'm not about to be strapped with a kid and wife. You, of all people, should have figured that out."

"Believe me, I thought long and hard about telling you. But this baby is yours, as much as I rue that fact. And I thought you should know."

"So, now I know." He raked a hand through his hair, then shook his head. "Hell, Jilly. I need some time to think about things. And talk to an attorney, I guess."

"Do whatever you need to do," she said, suddenly sorry she'd listened to Jeff's advice. She could have saved herself a ton of humiliation by keeping her secret. "I'm not happy about this, either. I'm going to owe the poor child a ton of apologies, since he or she is getting the short end of the stick in the father department."

Undaunted by her slam, he merely shrugged. "I'm going to ask for a paternity test."

"Whatever." She turned on her heel and strode for

the door, eager to escape the man she should never have gotten involved with in the first place.

Before she could turn the knob, he caught her arm and pulled her around to face him.

His usually cocky stance slumped and a bit of remorse softened his expression. "Listen, Jilly. I'm sorry about being a jerk, but you're going to have to give me some time to think things through."

She could certainly understand his need to think things through, and she tried to understand his shock and frustration. But that didn't make him any less of a jerk. "The news didn't sit well with me, either."

"Don't get your hopes up, Jilly. I'm not going to offer marriage."

Did he think that she wanted to marry him? That marriage to him would solve all her problems?

She raised her chin, mustering all the bravado she could find. "Don't worry about me being disappointed, Cain. Being married to a guy like you would be an awful penance to pay for past mistakes."

She just hoped his involvement in her child's future wouldn't be worse.

Jeff and his crew climbed from the plane and dispersed on the temporary landing field after another day of dousing the flames that continued to threaten Custer National Forest.

Exhausted and tired of sucking smoke and ash into his lungs, Jeff took one last look at the C-130 transport plane that had been converted to a tanker. At twenty-four, he was pretty damn young to be flying one of the big birds, and he knew it. But not many guys his age could boast of his extensive experience.

The U.S. Forestry Service had been surprised at the cockpit proficiency he'd garnered in his youth, but they quickly put him to use as a pilot for MAFFS when he'd been hired.

Jeff had always loved planes and flying, and on his fifteenth birthday, his uncle Stratton took him to the airfield and paid for his first ride in a biplane. It had been the best gift he'd ever had and had merely whetted his appetite for more flights, more time in the air.

It wasn't every teenager who could afford his own flying lessons in a multitude of different planes, nor every kid who had the good fortune of meeting a guy like Hank Ragsdale at an air show in Billings.

Hank had taken young Jeff under his wing and introduced him to other members of the Commemorative Air Force, a host of airmen who flew old World War II planes. Jeff had earned his pilot's license at the age of sixteen, and from then on out, there was no stopping him—not with the money in the hefty trust fund that his mother had left him.

Jeff had been certified in more planes than he could count, thanks to Hank and his buddies.

"Forsythe," Jim Anderson called from the make-shift command post. "How'd it go today?"

"Not bad. But we've got a lot of work ahead of us." Jeff lifted the bill of his hat and raked a hand through his hair. It had been a hell of a long day already. "Are we making any progress out near Rocky Point?"

"I'm afraid not." Jim furrowed his brow. "In fact, a couple of firemen from Rumor sent to assist us are missing. We're going to send a Huey out to search for them now."

Jeff's first concern was for his cousin, Reed Kingsley, the Rumor Fire Chief. "Who's out there?"

"Harry Willett and Cain Kincaid. They were having radio trouble earlier, so I'm not sure what's going on."

*Cain.*

Jeff's heart dropped to his gut. He might want to pound the guy senseless, but he didn't want anything—other than a good and well-deserved beating—to happen to the father of Jilly's baby. "Who's going to look for them?"

Jim nodded toward a CH1 single-engine with the blades rotating. "Bart Henthorne. That's him heading out."

"I'm going with him," Jeff said.

"Now wait a minute. You've been out all day, Forsythe. Take a break."

Jeff shook his head. "This is personal, Jim. Cain is a friend of a friend."

"Oh, what the hell. Go ahead. Just don't get heroic. If you need a rescue team, radio in and we'll send one out. I don't want anything happening to you."

Jeff shot his boss a grin. "I'll be fine. Don't worry about me."

Then he loped toward the Huey, intending to reach the chopper before it took off.

Jeff hadn't liked Cain Kincaid since the first grade. The guy had always been a braggart and a liar. And Jeff couldn't believe it had taken Jilly so long to see through him.

"He comes from a nice family," she'd said in the fireman's defense.

"Yeah?" Jeff had responded. "Well his parents gave him a biblical name he's certainly living up to."

Jilly had figured his status as a public servant in the community gave his character some sort of validation. But a snake in the grass like Cain didn't grow legs and feet, just because he was slithering through life in a uniform.

The weekly talks Jeff and Jilly had shared only confirmed his opinion. In fact, each time Jilly revealed more about her relationship with the fireman, Jeff's list of mental grievances against the guy grew.

When Jilly's car was in the shop, Cain forgot to pick her up at work—not once but twice. He borrowed money from her, then had a million excuses why he couldn't pay her back.

Cain even skipped out on caring for her when she got the flu, telling her he didn't want to catch the bug and then going out with the guys to Beauty and the Beats, the strip joint, instead. "Hey, babe," he'd told

Jilly. "It was a guy thing. Those girls can't hold a candle to you."

Yeah, right.

At least twice Cain cheated on her in the four months they'd dated. Knowing the Rumor Romeo's reputation, Jeff suspected Jilly had only managed to catch him twice.

But Cain was the father of Jilly's baby, and Jeff was determined to bring the man to safety and encourage him to do right by her, even if doing right only meant providing financial support.

"I'm coming with you," Jeff said to Bart Henthorne, as he climbed into the chopper. "Let's go find those guys."

For nearly twenty minutes the pilot and Jeff scoured the perimeter of the fire line, searching for the firefighters who'd lost radio contact with the command post.

The hot, smoky air swirled around them, at times clouding their vision as they scanned rocks, trees and mountainsides, looking for the yellow suits of the missing men. Their last-known position was a half mile from Rocky Point, a rugged mountain that had been aptly named by early trappers and settlers.

"There they are," the chopper pilot said, pointing to the left. "On the east side of Rocky Point."

One man was sprawled on the ground, obviously injured. The other stood, waving his arms.

"Damn," the pilot said. "That fire is pretty close. We'd better get a rescue crew out here."

And the fire would soon box them in. Jeff didn't think a rescue team could make it in time. "We've got to get them now."

"There's no place for me to land," the chopper pilot said. "And at this altitude, power is going to be a problem. We're not equipped to do a rescue."

"We'll have to try. My first job with the forestry service was working on a rescue team. I know the drills backward and forward. And since we don't have a crewman, I'll go down. Can you run the hoist?"

"Yeah, but it's going to be tricky." The pilot shook his head. "I don't know about this, Jeff. This bird isn't equipped with all the rescue gear. And I'm at max power now. If I start losing turns, we'll all go down."

"I'll try and make this quick."

"The winds are pretty damn gusty. Be careful."

Jeff strapped himself into the horse collar and descended from the hovering aircraft. The rotating blades sent the hot, smoky air swirling around him as the cable lowered him to the small patch of rocky ground where the stranded firemen waited.

A quick glance told him the wounded man was Cain. Blood and dirt covered the side of his head and face. And his eyes were closed.

"Is he alive?" Jeff asked Willett, voice straining to be heard over the noise of the chopper.

"Just barely. A burning tree limb fell on him, knocking him out. I dragged him this far, hoping to reach the rocky spot where we could escape the flames. We lost the radio somewhere along the way."

"We'll get you out of here," Jeff said. "But let's load him on the litter."

Willett helped Jeff guide the basket that would carry Cain to the safety of the chopper.

Before lifting the wounded man onto the litter, Jeff looked him over. He had a knot the size of a golf ball over his eye, and a ragged gash gaped at the left temple. Blood, ash and dirt didn't hide a third-degree burn on his cheek.

Jeff felt for a pulse and got one. As they loaded Cain onto the basket, he came to and grimaced in pain. Maybe the injured fireman would be all right, once they got him to Whitehorn Memorial Hospital.

When they'd secured Cain to the litter, Jeff told Willett to go first. With the pilot controlling the chopper and the hoist, they'd need someone to help pull Cain to safety.

As Jeff prepared to signal Willet they were ready to go, Cain opened his eyes. His pain-filled gaze fixed on Jeff. "Thanks for coming after us, Forsythe."

"It's my job."

Cain nodded, his pale face twisted in pain and his voice hoarse. "Am I gonna make it?"

"You'd better make it," Jeff said. "You've got a kid on the way. And some responsibility to face." Jeff signaled the pilot to pull the basket up.

When it was Jeff's turn, he grabbed the line to ascend. Smoke swirled around him, burning his throat and stinging his eyes, while the wind swung his cable high and wide. The chopper struggled to stay steady, but as Jeff left the ground, dangling like bait on the line, an updraft jerked the helicopter, slamming him against a rock on the mountainside.

He heard the sound of his bone breaking before feeling a sharp crack of pain and a brutal ache that made his head spin, but he managed to hold on to consciousness. He swung out of control, all the while trying desperately to stay alert, to ignore smoke in his eyes and lungs, the excruciating pain in his head, arm and shoulder.

When he'd first started this flight, he'd told Henthorne he knew the rescue routine backward and forward. He just hoped the chopper pilot could manage to fly without using the guillotine switch that would cut the cable, thus saving those on board and the bird.

A couple of times he felt the buzz that came with loss of consciousness, yet somehow he managed to stay coherent. It seemed like hours before the hoist began to pull him up.

As he was dragged onto the chopper floor, Jeff asked Willett, "How's Kincaid?"

But before he could hear the answer, a throbbing roar filled his ears and darkness settled around him.

# *Chapter Four*

The next afternoon Jilly worked on a funeral spray of pink carnations for Mildred Sanderson, an elderly woman whose memorial service would be held at the Rumor Community Church on Friday morning.

The bell on the door chimed, and she looked up to see Blake Cameron enter the florist shop, his tattered, gray backpack slung over his shoulder.

What was it about the kid that tweaked her sympathy? Maybe it was because he reminded her of Jeff, although just in looks and temperament. Jeff had been born to a life of privilege, and Blake was strictly blue-collar.

She smiled at the dark-haired teen whose life, she suspected, was not much better than hers had been. "If you want an after-school snack, I've got doughnuts in the back room."

The munchies, unfortunately, had struck again. But

she guessed her increasing weight and girth were no longer a major concern, so this morning she'd given in to the craving for chocolate éclairs and glazed doughnuts from the MonMart bakery.

"Sure. I'm always hungry, or so my dad says." The teen wandered to the back of the shop and returned with a broom in one hand and a glazed twist in the other.

Jilly continued to work, clipping the stem of a pink carnation and sticking it into the spray she was making. She cocked her head. Maybe the flower should rest a tad lower.

In the background, the soft sounds of classy elevator music blended with the gentle swoosh and scratch of a broom on scarred hardwood floors, as the teenager she'd hired as a delivery boy swept the shop.

Blake slowly made his way to the worktable where she stood. "Did you hear the news?"

She placed a sprig of baby's breath into the spray of carnations. "What news? I don't hear much of anything these days."

"The wind shifted yesterday afternoon, and a couple of Rumor firemen fighting the forest fire near Rocky Point were cut off from the dirt road by the flames. They sent in a rescue chopper to get them out, but one man died from his injuries."

Jilly's heart did a nosedive. Cain was fighting that fire. And so were some of the other guys she'd met through him. "Do you know who it was?"

Blake mumbled, pointing to his mouth and indicating the need to finish chewing before he could answer her question.

"Yeah," he said, jaws still moving. "The dead guy lived in my apartment complex. His name was Cain, but I don't know the last name. I only saw him a time or two."

She dropped the carnation in her hand and grabbed ahold of the table to steady herself. Obviously, Blake didn't know she'd been involved with Cain in a romantic way. "Are you sure? He's dead?"

"Yep. Reed Kingsley, the fire chief, came by the apartments and talked to the manager. I was standing right there and heard it all."

Jilly glanced at the funeral spray she was making. Cain, who loved life—maybe too much—was gone. She would be creating arrangements and sprays for his memorial service in the next few days.

A sense of sadness washed over her, yet her heart felt surprisingly numb.

Her baby's father—her old lover—was dead. Shouldn't she be feeling something? Grief? Heartbreak?

Would she mourn later? When reality set in? When the community hosted a funeral service?

She closed her eyes, her hand reaching to the small bulge in her tummy where her baby grew, warm, protected and completely unaware of the tragic circumstances surrounding his or her birth.

Jilly would bear her child alone, a single mother to the fullest extent of the definition.

She might have told Jeff that she didn't need Cain or his financial support, but now that she couldn't depend on either, doubt crept into her mind.

Money couldn't buy happiness, the old adage said, but it could sure take the edge off misery better than poverty could. And she ought to know; she'd had her share of both misery and poverty.

Jilly planned to offer her children more than her parents had provided her. She wanted her kids to have a sense of stability, hope for the future.

Her son or daughter would have a real house, not a run-down trailer like the one in which she'd lived while growing up. Her child would play on a swing set perched on a green lawn and surrounded by a picket fence, not a rusted-out sedan that no longer ran and was encircled by overgrown weeds.

Her child would come home from school to the scent of cookies baking in the oven, not stale cigarette smoke and beer.

But was a loving home all she could offer her baby?

What about her dream of being a part of the Rumor community, maybe even president of the PTA someday? She'd fought long and hard to earn respectability. Would bearing a child out of wedlock wipe out all she'd accomplished?

Or had Jilly—like her mother, Jo-Ellen Davis— set the circumstances in motion that would lead her back to a no-account life? Especially since Jilly had never managed to feel as if she'd truly broken free and become an accepted, respectable member of the Rumor community.

Until recently.

So close, yet so far away.

Jilly reached for a carnation and fingered the stem. If Rumor had tracks, she would have been born on the wrong side of them. In fact, she'd probably still be living on the outskirts of town and the fringe of society if it hadn't been for Jeff.

Most folks hadn't understood what Carolyn Kingsley's nephew had seen in the little Davis girl. And why not?

Jeff's mother had been a wealthy socialite—East Coast born and bred. And Jilly had grown up with very little supervision or kindness—other than what she'd received from the McDonough family who had lived next door.

She thought of Emmy McDonough, her one-time best friend and neighbor, and Emmy's two older brothers whom Jilly had once looked up to.

Karl had gone off to fight in the Gulf War, and Ash went to prison. In a way, the McDonough boys had let Jilly down, just as they had their little sister.

The only guy in her life who had stuck around had been Jeff.

And he'd been there through all her trials and tribulations, including her mother's death.

Jilly had only been seventeen when she came home to find her mother dead, the victim of an apparent suicide. It had been Jeff she called first, to wait with her for the coroner to arrive. And it had been Jeff who'd listened to her cry and bemoan the fact her mother had let her down yet again.

Sometimes Jilly's lot in life seemed to be her own fault, directly or indirectly. Even her mother's choice to check out of life because her latest man was a bigger loser than the last had felt like Jilly's fault... somehow.

It had been Jeff who'd convinced her otherwise.

And Jeff who had always been there for her.

Jilly blew out a sigh. There wasn't much he could do to protect her from herself or the mess she'd made of her life this time.

"Mr. Kingsley was pretty cool," Blake said, as he popped the rest of the doughnut in his mouth. "When I asked him some questions about the fire and the rescue of the men, he took time to answer me. And I know he's gotta be really busy right now, with the fire and all."

Jilly had no doubt Reed was busy. He still had to provide fire protection for the town, while giving up some of his men.

"I told him I might take that fire-fighting course they offer at the community college in Billings."

"That sounds like a great career move, if you want to be a fireman."

"Yeah, that's what I thought. But I might like to be a pilot and work with MAFFS, just like Mr. Kingsley's cousin."

Jilly smiled, her heart filling with pride at Jeff's

accomplishments. When he set his mind to something, he did it. And he'd always said he was going to fly planes, not just turbo props, but anything that left the ground. And he had.

Blake licked the glaze from his fingers. "Jeff—that's his cousin's name—was part of the search team that found the stranded firemen, then had to rescue them."

"Oh, really?" Jilly asked, her curiosity piqued. Jeff had flown with chopper rescue teams in the past, but from what she understood, he flew the C-130s exclusively now.

"Yeah. Mr. Kingsley was heading to the hospital in Whitehorn when he left."

"Why is that?" Jilly asked.

"That's where they took Jeff, after he was injured during the rescue."

Jilly dropped the carnation she'd been holding. "Jeff was hurt?"

"Yeah, pretty bad, but Mr. Kingsley said he'd be all right. He just won't be able to fly for a while."

Jeff had been injured, badly enough to land in the hospital. Her heart pounded in her ears. "Listen, Blake. You're going to have to close up for me. I've got to go into Whitehorn."

Jilly rushed through the lobby doors of Whitehorn Memorial Hospital, stopping just long enough to ask the volunteers at the front desk where she could find Jeff Forsythe.

In room 204, she was told.

She must have been white as a sheet when she strode through the door of his room, because the first words out of Jeff's mouth were, "Jilly? Are you all right?"

"Me?" She studied the wounded man lying in bed, his arm in a castlike thing, a white, bulky bandage on the side of his head. "Look at you."

"This?" He nodded at his arm. "Just a little inconvenience, that's all. You're the one I'm worried about. Shoot, Jilly, I don't know anything about pregnant women, but I'd think flying into my room like a demon out of hell wouldn't do you or the baby any good."

"Why didn't you call me?"

"I wasn't conscious until this morning. Then they stuck me in ICU for a while, as a precaution. I just got into this room about twenty minutes ago. I called the shop and talked to some kid who said he worked for you."

She crossed her arms, willing her heart to still and her nerves to settle down, but to no avail. "What happened?"

The expression on his face grew pensive, and he paused, as though struggling to find the right words. "Cain was injured—critically."

"I heard." Her voice came out soft, like a whisper. She tried to feel something, to react. To cry. But for some reason, she'd lost Cain a long time ago. And her tears had already been spent.

"He didn't make it, honey."

She merely nodded, a flood of emotions swirling in her mind. Had the grief finally surfaced? She wasn't sure, but she hoped so.

Again guilt reared its head, forcing her to face the fact that she'd been far more affected by Jeff's injury than Cain's death.

What kind of heartless person was she?

Cain was her baby's father, her old lover. She'd cared for him once. Deeply. He might have reacted badly yesterday, but he would have come around with time. Probably.

She placed a hand upon her womb, caressing the baby and offering comfort, or so it seemed.

Jeff studied her with sorrow-filled eyes, suggesting that he thought he'd somehow failed her. "I tried to bring him home—"

Jilly sat in the chair beside Jeff's bed, then trailed her fingers along his cheek. "I heard that you were part of the rescue team."

"I'm sorry," he said again. "We did what we could."

"I know."

Why couldn't she cry? Show some compassion for her child's father, her one-time lover?

She'd been angry when she last talked to Cain, yet she didn't feel anger right now—or grief—just an overwhelming numbness. Normally she'd been able to share everything with Jeff. But not this weird sense of nothing.

"How long will you be here?" she asked.

"They're keeping me for observation until tomorrow morning, although I suspect it's only because my aunt is on the hospital board and was so insistent." He rolled his eyes as though embarrassed by Carolyn Kingsley's connections.

"I imagine she's still recovering from the scare she had last December when your cousin Russell was in that coma. A head injury is pretty serious stuff."

"Maybe so, but other than a headache and a couple stitches, I'm fine."

"And the arm?"

He glanced at the castlike covering. "Broken, but it will heal."

Jilly knew this wasn't the first time Jeff had been subject to his aunt's well-meaning concern. And she knew how Jeff managed to rebel, although usually in a passive-aggressive way.

She'd never been able to understand his rebellion, though. She would have felt privileged to be part of the Kingsley family and would have done everything she could to stay in their good graces.

"I would have put up a fuss about staying here overnight," Jeff confessed, "if I didn't have to recover back at the ranch. My aunt has always hovered around me, and I figured we'd both be happier if I remained here. I can kick the nurses out of my room, but I don't like hurting Aunt Carolyn's feelings."

"Your mom was her only sister," Jilly reminded him. Gosh, what she wouldn't give to have a family who cared that much about her.

"I don't think my aunt ever got over losing my mom."

Jilly didn't think Jeff had, either, but she kept her observation to herself. "Is that why you flew the coop so young?"

"Yep." He blew out a sigh. "That's the main reason. I care about my family and appreciate everything they've done for me, but I've never felt like a real part of them. And I probably never will."

If Jilly had a family like the Kingsleys—heck, if she had a family at all—she'd be happy to let them hover around her. And she would *never* fly the coop.

But Jeff was different. Like a hawk in the wild, he loved the freedom of flight. A cage would kill him. No one understood that better than Jilly.

She tossed him a smile. "When they release you, why not come home with me? I promise not to hover around you."

Go home with Jilly?

Now, that was an idea. Not that Jeff needed her to fuss over him. She was the one in need of a friend and a shoulder to lean on. He could see how broken up she was.

She might not have shed a tear in front of him, but red, puffy eyes revealed her grief and announced she'd cried all the way to the hospital. It had been a rough couple of days for her, first finding out about an unplanned and untimely pregnancy, then losing Cain.

Nobody knew Jilly the way he did. She might

have a tough exterior, but it only masked her vulnerability.

And she was vulnerable right now, more so than she'd ever been.

Jeff glanced at his arm and realized he'd be on disability for a while and unable to fly. The thought of being grounded in Rumor had always made him uneasy, but what would a week or two hurt?

Jilly needed him. Maybe with his help she could sort through the changes in her life.

"I think I'll take you up on the offer. I'd like to stay at your house." Jeff pushed the button that would call the nurse.

"Yes?" a faceless voice responded.

"I want to check out of here."

"But, sir," the voice over the intercom responded, "your aunt…I mean, the doctor wants you to stay until tomorrow morning."

"Get me whatever forms I need to sign. I want to be released, or I'm walking out on my own."

"Very well," the voice said.

Jilly frowned and reached for his hand, circling her thumb softly against his skin. "Are you sure about this? Maybe you should stay."

Her concern touched him, easing a bit of the frustration he felt at being stuck in Rumor. "Don't worry. I'm okay."

When the nurse came in, lips pulled tight and smug, she lifted a hypodermic needle.

"What's that for?" Jeff asked.

"Pain. Dr. Kendrick said you'd probably be asking for medication all through the night. That was a bad break. And if you insist upon leaving, I want to make sure the ride home isn't unbearable."

"All right." Jeff offered her his uninjured arm, willing to appease the woman as long as she didn't fight him on checking out of the hospital.

"Sorry," the mousy-haired woman said. "But this needs to go in your buttocks."

Oh, great.

The nurse whipped the curtain around, although so quickly, Jeff wondered if she'd blocked out Jilly's view. But he wasn't about to whine about it and rolled to the left, letting her at his backside.

Had Jilly turned away to give him even more privacy? Or had she merely ignored the procedure?

Of course, Jilly never had been one to ignore his discomfort. A smile curved his lips, but only until the needle jabbed his skin. The nurse, it seemed, had struck with a vengeance.

"Now, ma'am," Jeff said through a grimace, "would you please get my clothes, as well as my walking papers? I'm getting out of here."

Jeff sat in the passenger seat of Jilly's sedan, his arm propped on a pillow Jilly had taken from his hospital bed, his head resting lightly against the neckrest.

It felt weird going home with her, and not just

because of the shot of legal dope that left him rheumy and a bit goofy.

He didn't like being out of commission—physically or mentally.

"Doesn't this kind of make you feel like Bonnie and Clyde?" Jilly glanced across the car and flashed him a smile.

"Because you stole a pillow I'm going to get charged a hundred dollars for?"

"Well, yes. And because I busted you out. Now I'm driving the getaway car."

"Well, don't get any ideas about robbing any banks until I'm back to fighting weight." Jeff closed his eyes, not at all liking the side effects of the pain medication.

And to think, some people actually enjoyed this surreal feeling.

"Are you okay?" Jilly asked, her eyes darting back and forth between him and the road. "You don't look very good."

"I'd rather be in pain." Jeff rolled his eyes and blew out a sigh. "Why'd I agree to that damn shot?"

Jilly chuckled. "I'm not sure, probably because you're not as rebellious as me. I would have told that crotchety nurse where to stick that needle."

"I don't doubt that for a minute." Jeff managed a smile, in spite of his body and mind being in the twilight zone.

"But I have to admit I'm glad you gave in and rolled over."

"Why's that?"

"You've got a great butt, flyboy. And this lucky girl got a peek."

He shot a glance across the seat. "You peeked through the curtain?"

She giggled, and although he had half a notion to scold her, knowing she'd appreciated his bare backside did something to him.

Something even the pain medicine couldn't alter.

"I've got a great butt, huh?"

She slid him a naughty-girl smile that made his blood pump where it shouldn't.

It was the medication, he reminded himself. It had him thinking all kinds of goofy things.

As Jilly pulled into her driveway, Jeff blew out a sigh of relief. Maybe if he just lay down for a while and took a nap, he'd wake feeling himself again.

Jilly strode around the Taurus and opened the passenger door. "Let me help you into the house."

"I'll be okay." But when he tried to stand, he slumped against the car door.

Jilly wrapped his good arm around her shoulder, then slowly led him into the house. In spite of himself, he leaned into her, felt her soft and gentle curves, caught a fresh whiff of her floral scent.

A guy could get used to being a fifty-pound weakling, if he had a woman like Jilly to take care of him.

Again he blamed the medication and reprimanded

himself for letting his thoughts run in a sexual direction. This was his best friend, for cripe's sake. Nothing more, nothing less.

When they stepped inside the living room, a dog barked and howled. The automated dust mop was probably locked in the broom closet.

"I'll be right there," Jilly called. "Hang on just a minute, Posey."

"Where is she?"

"On the service porch. It's safer to leave her there while I'm gone. She's still in that puppy stage and likes to chew."

Jeff nodded toward the sofa. "Just let me lie down here."

"Nothing doing. You're going to use my bed. I'll take the sofa."

He wanted to argue, but he didn't have the strength. Jilly could be stubborn when she had her mind set on something.

Posey cried out again, as Jilly led Jeff down a narrow hall to the bedroom and pulled back a white, goose-down comforter, revealing lavender sheets.

Jilly had the kind of bed that welcomed a weary soul.

And a willing lover.

Had Cain slept with her here? Held her close?

Jeff struggled with jealousy…or something damn near like it. And he cursed under his breath.

"Did I hurt you?"

"No. I'm fine." His words came out harsher than

he'd intended. "Thanks for letting me stay here tonight."

"I'm glad to help."

He turned to sit on the edge of the mattress, but his foot caught on something, a floor rug, maybe. He fell to the bed, taking Jilly with him.

Fortunately he managed to hold his injured arm out of the way, which protected it to an extent, but didn't prevent a throbbing stab of pain.

He winced. "Damn it."

"Are you okay?" she asked, arms braced on each side of him, her body covering his. She didn't move. She lay there, heart pounding against his chest, eyes fixed on his.

He might be pretty much out of it, but it seemed that something passed between them, some knowledge or awareness. Hell, he didn't know what it was, but it was enough to keep them from moving or breaking eye contact.

"Yeah," he said, trying to gain some kind of control over himself. "I'm fine."

But was he?

The soft, fullness of her breasts pressed against his chest. Her scent—an earthy, floral bouquet that he doubted was perfume—settled around him.

Unable to help himself, he stroked her back with his good arm. His pulse quickened, and his body reacted in the way nature had intended.

Had she noticed?

"Let me get off," she said, her voice as soft and velvety as a lover's caress.

Get off? The thought of her climaxing only made him grow harder.

Yet she didn't move right away, and he didn't force the issue. Maybe she enjoyed the contact as much as he had.

The little dog howled again and this time scratched at the door.

"I'd better go check on Posey before she goes crazy."

Then Jilly slowly eased away, leaving Jeff longing for more than her compassion or comfort.

## *Chapter Five*

Jilly didn't sleep well, but she couldn't blame the narrow, living-room sofa or the hot summer night. Having Jeff under her roof—and in her bed—had kept her mind humming until nearly dawn.

She tried to tell herself that the pleasure flooding her heart was due to having her good friend around and having the opportunity to take care of him for a change, to pay back all he'd done for her in the past. Wasn't that the reason she'd left his door slightly ajar—so she could hear him call out if he needed her?

But it was more than that.

She liked having company and knowing someone was just down the hall, which was weird, she supposed, since she'd spent so much time fending for herself as a child and should be used to solitude.

Then again, maybe it wasn't so odd after all.

She'd always wanted to fit in, to belong, to be a part of the community, a part of a family. And in spite of her tough-girl act, and as much as she hated to admit it, she disliked being alone.

Two months ago, when she'd found Posey on her floral shop doorstep, dirty and whimpering from hunger and neglect, it wasn't just a sympathetic and tender heart that had compelled her to adopt the little dog.

Taking in the stray had been the first step toward building her home, creating a family.

She placed a hand on her tummy, felt the place where her baby grew. Would her love for the child be enough? There was so much she wanted to give her son or daughter—a house, a yard, a dog.

A mommy who would do whatever it took to provide her child with a loving home was a start, she supposed, but would it be enough?

Deep inside, she'd always dreamed about providing her children with a parent who'd garnered community respect and acceptance, something she'd never had growing up.

But sometimes she thwarted her own efforts, or so it seemed.

Being an unwed mother had never been part of her game plan, and she worried about what the good folks of Rumor would say behind her back.

She'd find out soon enough.

The morning sun peered through a slit in the

living-room blinds, bearing evidence that dawn had broken.

More than once, Jilly had awakened in the middle of the night to check on Jeff. Each time she entered the bedroom, saw his large, muscular body sprawled on her double bed, an odd sense of sexual curiosity muscled to the forefront, shoving friendly concern to the side.

Last night when Jilly had tried to help Jeff to the bed, she'd actually fallen on him, landed breast to chest, eye to eye. And much to her surprise, she'd found herself stimulated, turned on.

Had it been her imagination? Or had he hardened underneath her?

"Oh, for Pete's sake," she muttered. Those were the kind of crazy thoughts that had kept her tossing and turning on the narrow sofa.

She needed to get this…this awkward sense of lust under control. Jeff was her best friend, and he'd be leaving soon—if not today.

Jilly folded her blanket and put it away. After letting Posey out in the backyard to do doggie business, she wandered down the hall to check on Jeff again, to ask how he'd slept, see whether he needed anything.

But something more than compassion urged her onward, something she refused to analyze.

A growing sense of curiosity nipped at her heels until she reached the bedroom and slowly pushed open the door. She poked her head inside and found the hunk awake, lying on his back, his broken arm propped on a pillow, dark hair rumpled from sleep, a slow smile tugging at his lips.

Her bed had never looked so good, so appealing. And neither had her friend.

"Good morning," she said, her voice bearing a husky tone, which she hoped Jeff would blame on the sandman. She knew better, since she'd been awake for nearly an hour. "Did you sleep well?"

"Not too bad, under the circumstances. Whatever was in that shot knocked me for a loop."

She tucked a loose strand of hair behind her ear, wondering why she hadn't run a brush through the sleep-tousled mop. "Hungry?"

"Yeah," he said, stretching like a mountain lion on a rock ledge in the sun. "But I'd like a shower first."

She nodded toward the arm he had propped on a pillow. "Are you allowed to get that wet?"

"Probably not. Do you have a trash bag? I can wrap it in plastic and keep it dry."

"Sure," she said, although she remained still. She didn't want to walk away, head to the kitchen for a green plastic bag. Not now. Not while her feminine fascination was taking hold.

Even wounded, Jeff held an alluring appeal.

He threw off the covers and sat up, grimacing as he did so. "I might need some help, though."

Help? An image of her undressing him came to

mind, helping him remove his shirt, unbutton the pants he still wore.

The strange, sexual fantasy took an interesting twist, as water sprayed from the shower spigot and steam swirled around them. She and Jeff stepped under the warm water, naked, hands reaching, mouths—

For goodness' sake, her imagination needed a dressing down. *Oops.* Wrong choice of words.

Jeff swung his denim-clad legs over the edge of the mattress. He hadn't undressed last night, and since he mentioned needing a nap, she hadn't suggested it. But he'd slept until morning.

"If you can get the snaps and buttons undone," he said, "I can do the rest."

A naughty smile curled her lips. "I'd be happy to, flyboy. Need some help washing your back?"

He chuckled and shook his head, assuming, she supposed, that she was joking. And she was.

Sort of.

"Just the buttons, ma'am."

Minutes later they stood in the small bathroom, water running and steam building. A white fluffy towel and a green trash bag sat on the pink-speckled tile countertop.

Jilly unbuttoned Jeff's shirt, trying hard not to take her time, not to splay her hands upon his bare chest, not to skim her fingers along his tanned skin.

Self-control held, but just barely.

As she unsnapped the top metal button on his

jeans, her knuckles brushed against the hairline that ran downward from his navel. Her breath caught, her fingers fumbled and her heart pounded in her chest.

If he noticed her virginal reaction, he didn't mention it.

Instead, he tugged gently on a strand of her hair. "Thanks, Jilly. I can take it from here."

She nodded. "Call me if you need anything."

He seemed to ponder her words, his needs. "I'll be fine."

"Good." She offered him a smile.

Then with more regret than was proper, she left him to shower alone.

Jilly fixed a breakfast of ham and eggs. When they'd both eaten, she showered and dressed for work.

Before leaving, she showed Jeff her video library and gave him a great book she'd just finished reading—a *New York Times* bestselling suspense novel.

Then she let Posey into the house. "Keep an eye on the patient, will you, girl?"

"You're asking a dog to baby-sit me?"

"Would you rather go out to the ranch? Your aunt and uncle have a whole staff to look after you."

"No, thanks," he answered rather quickly. "I don't need a caretaker, but thanks for the reminder. I'd better let Aunt Carolyn know I'm okay before she finds out that I left the hospital. Knowing her, she'd call the sheriff and report me as a missing person."

"You should definitely call. I sure don't want to be charged with kidnapping. Or aiding and abetting a fugitive." Jilly laughed, then slipped her purse over her shoulder. She paused before opening the front door. "I'll be home this afternoon, as soon as Blake arrives at the shop and can relieve me. Just make yourself at home."

"Don't worry about me," Jeff said.

She hadn't worried, not really.

But her thoughts remained on him all day long. Several times she called home, although she wasn't entirely sure why.

Did she want to check on him?

Or make sure he was still at her house?

She refused to contemplate the questions. And labeled the phone calls friendly concern.

But her concern didn't please him after the third call. "Thanks to you and Aunt Carolyn, the phone has been ringing off the hook," Jeff said, "and I can't get any peace and quiet. I told you I was doing just fine."

The next time she had the urge to call, she lied and told him she was worried about Posey. Had he taken the dog out for her doggie business?

He grumbled, which led her to believe he'd forgotten poor Posey completely, then said, "I thought you said that little mutt was looking after me."

As morning drew to a close and afternoon wore

on, Jilly tried her best to get everything done so that her teenage helper was left with little to do other than answer the phone and write down orders for flower arrangements.

At times like this she was glad she'd hired Blake. When he'd first knocked at her florist-shop door, asking for work, she hadn't needed an employee, nor could she really afford one.

But there was something about the high-school honor student that burrowed into her heart when he stood before her, proud, yet eyes begging. So she'd hired him, knowing her accountant would scold her.

But if the truth were known, she liked having someone to chat with during the day, even on a part-time basis.

Last week the kid had purchased his own vehicle, a beat-up old Plymouth that was more primer gray than the powder blue it had once been painted.

Jilly had been thrilled for him. No one understood the sense of self-satisfaction that came from providing for oneself more than she did.

At four, Blake came in, tattered backpack slung over his shoulder. Thankful that reinforcements had arrived, Jilly hurried to clean up her worktable so she could go home.

"I hope it's okay with you," Blake said, "but I'm going to have to leave early today. My dad has the late shift this evening, and he's having car trouble again."

Car trouble? Jilly couldn't help but wonder if that was the truth, since it was common knowledge that Mr. Cameron had his driver's license suspended a while back for some reason.

There were two versions of the local gossip. One suggested an outrageous amount of back child support as the reason; the other blamed a couple of drunk-driving convictions. Either way, it really didn't matter to her.

Blake was a decent kid. It wasn't his fault that his old man was a loser, any more than it had been Jilly's fault that her mom couldn't find a stepfather who could keep a job or who seemed to care whether or not he had a paycheck.

After Jilly's dad skipped out on them, shortly after her fifth birthday, her mom brought a parade of men home to live. The last one had stayed the longest and been the one she remembered the most.

*Well, Jilly girl, looks like we're going out to dinner tonight. That soup kitchen in Whitehorn puts on a pretty good spread, don't you think? As soon as your mama and I finish our beer and have a cigarette, we'll leave.*

Jilly blew out a sigh. Blake had a rough row to hoe with his dad, but history didn't have to repeat itself. That was one of many lessons Jeff had taught her.

"Sure," she told the kid. "Go ahead and leave, if you need to."

Jilly had really wanted to go home early and see

about Jeff. She glanced at the clock, then scanned the shop.

What would it hurt to close up early? Take an hour or two off?

Probably not a gosh darn thing.

Leftovers and an old movie sounded like great fun, especially if Jeff was at home to share them with.

When Jeff heard Jilly's car drive up, he took Posey from his lap and put the wiggly little dust mop on the floor.

For some reason the dog had bonded with him over the course of the day. Jeff had never been an animal lover. When other kids asked for dogs, cats and a pony of their own, Jeff had begged for flight lessons or books and magazines on aircraft or flying.

But this little critter was kind of cute, in an ugly, bushy sort of way.

"You're home," Jilly said, as she let herself in the front door and spotted Jeff on the couch.

"Where did you think I'd be?"

She shrugged. "I don't know. Being cooped up in a house all day isn't your cup of herbal tea."

Jilly had that right. "Yeah, well I'm not staying home tomorrow."

Her expression grew serious. "Are you leaving?"

He'd have been long gone before now, if he hadn't been so worried about her. "I need to stick around for a while. Is it all right if I spend a few days with you?"

"Sure."

"But I'll sleep on the couch tonight. I'm not going to take your bed."

She smiled. "You may have to fight me for the sofa, flyboy. You're on injured reserve."

"Yeah, well, you're pregnant, so that puts both of us at a disadvantage."

Her smile fell, and he felt like a jerk for pointing out her condition, her situation. For reminding her of Cain.

Because he wasn't sure what to say, he kept his mouth shut. But he made his way toward her, slipped his good arm around her waist and pulled her close.

It had been the right thing to do, he supposed, because she leaned into him and wrapped her arms around his waist, fitting together with him like two pieces of a jigsaw puzzle. Her hair held the fragrance of peach shampoo, tempting him to take a deep breath and relish her scent.

She blew out a soft sigh. "I'm scared, Jeff."

He ran a hand along the gentle curve of her back, trying hard to offer his support. "What are you afraid of?"

"Everything." She took a deep breath and blew out another sigh, this one heavy and labored. "For one thing, the whole baby thing makes me nervous."

"You mean pregnancy and childbirth?" He couldn't help her much there.

She nodded. "Yeah, for starters. Then I have to

bring the baby home and be a mom, and I'm not sure what to do. I never had much of a role model."

She hadn't, he realized, thinking about Jo-Ellen Davis, a woman who'd been too wrapped up in her own sorry life to provide a loving home environment for her daughter.

His hand continued to caress Jilly's back in an effort to ease her mind. "Don't worry. You'll be a natural."

"Thanks for the vote of confidence." She pulled from his embrace, and his good arm fell reluctantly to the side.

"That baby will be lucky to have a mother like you," he said. And he meant it. Jilly eagerly poured herself into anything she attempted to do. Motherhood would be no different.

Her bottom lip quivered, as though she might cry, but she managed a crooked grin. "I never expected to have a baby without a husband."

"Life doesn't always happen the way we plan. It's what you do with the surprises that counts."

She walked toward the sofa and plopped down on the seat. Looking at him with cocker spaniel eyes, she asked, "What do you think the good folks of Rumor will think of me now?"

He joined her on the couch, not too close, not too far. "There might be a few old biddies who grumble and pass judgment, but you're a businesswoman and a homeowner, Jilly. No one who really counts is going to think badly of you."

"You count, Jeff." She tucked a strand of hair behind her ear and snagged his gaze. "What do you think of me?"

The earnestness of her question touched his heart. "I think you're going to be the best mom that ever walked the streets of Rumor."

"Walked the streets?" Her eyes narrowed and her lips tensed.

"That was a play on *walked the earth,* not a reference to street walking. Geez, Jilly, give me a break."

She blew out a soft, wobbly sigh. "You know, I've tried so hard to be accepted and respected. I don't want anyone to eye my baby the same way they used to look at me."

"They won't." Jeff wasn't sure what he was going to do to ensure Jilly's life would be as trouble free as she deserved, but he intended to give it his best shot. "I promise."

She looked at him, brown eyes skeptical, but she let the subject drop.

Two hours later, while they dined on leftover roast beef, potatoes and carrots, the phone rang, and Jilly answered.

She furrowed her brow and leaned her ear into the receiver, straining to hear, so it seemed. "Wait a second, Blake. Slow down and start over."

Jeff could only hear her side of the conversation, see her expression. She'd hired a teenager to help at the florist shop. His name was Blake, wasn't it?

She listened intently. "But I thought your dad had to work tonight—"

"Oh, sheesh," she muttered into the mouthpiece. "Don't worry. I'll be right there."

Then she hung up the phone and shook her head. "What did I do with my purse?"

"It's on the floor by the easy chair," Jeff said. "What's the matter?"

"I've got to go pick up Blake. His dad got into a jam, and the car won't start, and the sheriff is on his way—"

How many times had Jilly gotten in a jam and called Jeff? It looked as if she'd taken on that paternal role herself, and he smiled inwardly. "Where is he?"

She clicked her tongue and rolled her eyes. "He went to pick up his dad at Beauties and the Beat."

"The strip joint?"

"Yes, and Blake has a flat tire."

"You're not going after him."

"I have to. You don't understand. I'm the only one he can depend on. And he's underage." She looked at him with that soul-wrenching gaze that had always turned his better instincts to mush. Then she strode toward the easy chair for her purse.

Jeff grabbed her by the arm. "Now wait a minute. You're not going out there alone. I'm going with you."

"Oh, yeah?" Jilly asked arching a brow. "And if I need protecting, you're one fist short."

They were a pair, all right.

The loose cannon and the straight arrow.

Mutt and Jeff.

"Don't argue with me," he said, taking her hand and leading her out the door.

Jilly always seemed to find herself in one mess or another—most of them innocent mistakes. He'd tried to explain that to Aunt Carolyn when she'd questioned him about his friendship with a girl who seemed to always get him into trouble.

Carolyn Kingsley's regal expression had softened, and she'd reached out a hand to cup his cheek. "Jilly reminds you of your mother, doesn't she?"

Well, Jeff wouldn't go that far. It sounded a bit too much like that psychobabble the shrink would have suggested.

Jeff's mother, Jackie Forsythe, was the naughty society girl her sister worried over but adored. He imagined her older sister had come to her rescue a time or two.

And although he suspected his fun-loving mother would have liked Jilly, any similarity in this instance was really between Jeff and his aunt. They both tried to look out for the people they cared about.

And now he and Jilly, a woman who stirred feelings that weren't at all brotherly, were heading off on a mission of mercy to the strip joint.

He just hoped Aunt Carolyn didn't get wind of it.

## *Chapter Six*

Just past Rumor city limits, Jilly and Jeff rode in pensive silence along the darkened stretch of road that led to Beauties and the Beat.

Jilly had an urge to make light of their task, as she usually did when dragging him into one of her misadventures. But for some reason she didn't.

In the past she'd enjoyed teasing Jeff, pushing his patience to the limit, although she'd never been sure why.

Maybe it was a fun-loving attempt to draw a reaction from him. Or there was another possibility.

It could be that she enjoyed knowing someone cared enough to challenge her, to keep her in line. Either way, tonight was different. Jilly was stepping in as the hero, and Jeff was merely along for the ride.

At least, that's what she hoped.

Neither one of them were up for a bar fight, which is what Blake's dad had been involved in earlier. With no money to pay for damages, and a flat tire on Blake's car, the poor kid couldn't take his old man home.

The situation as Blake had relayed it on the phone stirred up best-forgotten memories that haunted Jilly like a goblin in the night.

As the Taurus passed the old trailer in which Jilly had once lived, each scene in her mind grew more vivid, the voices loud and clear.

*Jilly girl, bring me another beer, and while you're at it, straighten those rabbit ears on the TV. Wrestlin's on tonight. Gotta see ol' Fridge Freemont whoop the tar out of Treetop Turner.*

*But Ralph, Mrs. Corbin asked us to watch the news and report on a current event tomorrow.*

*Oh, hell, Jilly. Just make something up, will ya?*

Her foot pushed steadily down on the gas pedal. If Jeff noticed she'd accelerated, he didn't say a word.

Not far from the trailer, down the road and around the bend, a hot-pink stucco building stood alone, like a decrepit beacon that called lost souls home.

Inside, watered-down drinks and nearly naked girls awaited the lost and pointed them on the way to perdition.

Jilly, of all people, ought to know.

Her most recent stepdad, Ralph Edwards, had been a Friday- and Saturday-night regular and had complained often enough. Of course, neither weak drinks nor girls he considered overdressed in g-strings and pasties had kept Ralph away from his favorite hangout. Jilly and her mom had to drag him home from Beauties and the Beat more times than she could count. Each humiliating scene was engrained in her mind, the last one being the most vivid.

But that time, Jilly and her mom hadn't been called to take him home.

Apparently, someone had stumbled out the back door of the strip joint, only to find Ralph lying on the back steps, next to dented and rusted-out trash cans piled high to the point of overflowing with God only knew what kind of garbage that stunk to high heaven.

Jilly could still recall the dark night, the smoky haze that seemed to seep out of the windows and doors, creating an aura around the salmon-pink building. They'd arrived at the scene to find the flashing red lights of the sheriff's car and Ralph's body lying morbidly still in a puddle of blood.

He'd died as a result of blunt trauma to the head, the medical examiner had said. Possibly a tire iron. But no one was ever arrested for the murder, as far as Jilly knew.

To this day she always wondered whether it was because most people thought that the mouthy, obnoxious drunk had it coming.

They say a person doesn't miss what they never had, but Jilly knew exactly what she'd been lacking—a normal childhood.

As a kid, she got to experience fun family outings whenever Emmy's mom let her join them. Mom McDonough, as Jilly had always called her, had supplied the only decent family experience she'd ever known.

The tires of the Taurus crunched upon gravel as Jilly pulled into the darkened parking lot of the rundown dive. There weren't many spaces to choose from, but they managed to park close to Blake's car.

A slashed tire caused his old Plymouth to list to one side like a beached schooner.

She hoped Blake was okay and that she'd arrived in time. A quick scan of the parking lot told her the sheriff hadn't arrived. Which was a good thing, she supposed. He only seemed to show up for a felony offense.

Dangling from the front window of the strip joint, hanging crooked as though it were three sheets to the wind, a blue neon sign announced: XXX Dancers.

Triple X.

One day, while playing at Emmy's house, Jilly had asked Mom McDonough what XXX dancers meant. The single mother, who tried to do her best to raise good kids on her own, cleared her throat, then said, "Extra Large Dancers." A response that had satisfied both little girls.

When Jilly finally learned that XXX, in this case, didn't refer to a dress size, her respect for Emmy's mother had grown deeper.

Looking back, Jilly realized Mrs. McDonough had been a wonderful mother, even though a job that paid barely over minimum wage hadn't provided many extras for the family. It seemed as though the McDonough kids ate a lot of beans and rice, but the food was always tasty and filling, the conversation good-hearted and pleasant—a mother's love and sacrifice obvious.

Jilly placed a hand on her rounded tummy, hoping to be the same kind of mother to her child.

"Let's make this quick," Jeff said, as he opened the car door and slipped from the passenger's seat.

"Are you nuts?" Jilly asked.

"What are you talking about?"

"Do you think I want to hang out here any longer than necessary? This place gives me the willies, not to mention it brings back memories of childhood I can do without."

"I know." Jeff took Jilly's hand and gave it a squeeze. "But if you remember, about ten years ago you talked about getting a job here."

"It was a joke, just to get a rise out of you."

"Yeah, well, back then, this place held an adolescent appeal."

"And it doesn't any longer?"

*"Please,"* Jeff said. Then he flashed her a sexy grin. "Of course, it would probably get quite a rise out of me now, to see you dancing on that stage."

She swatted at his arm. "Just give me a few months

to fill out, then I'll really put on a show. Come on, let's go."

As Jeff led her into the dark, smoke-hazed dive, it took a while for her eyes to adjust. She had an urge to hold her breath so the fumes of cheap cigars, alcohol and stale sweat wouldn't harm her growing child. Of course, lack of oxygen wouldn't do the baby any good, either.

Jeff was right. They needed to make this quick.

She spotted Blake in a corner booth, his eyes wide—but not because he was gawking at the barely clad brunette who danced onstage and shimmied around a pole.

Instead, the kid watched as the short, heavyset proprietor shook a fist at his obviously intoxicated father. "You ain't leaving until I get paid, or the sheriff drags your sorry ass to jail."

"How much does he owe you?" Jilly asked.

The proprietor looked up, eyes sweeping her up and down. He smiled, causing the stub of a cigar to wiggle between clenched teeth, then slowly removed the offensive stump of tobacco from his mouth. "You're Ralph's kid, aren't you?"

Was that a badge of shame she'd have to carry the rest of her life, or only when she entered dives like this one?

"I'm Jilly Davis. How much does this man owe you?"

"Fifty-seven dollars, before he broke a chair against the bar. You payin' his tab?"

"Yes." Jilly reached into her purse and counted her bills. Forty-six dollars, more or less, even if she opened her change purse and dumped nickels, dimes and pennies onto the scarred Formica tabletop. She looked at Jeff. "I'm a little short."

"No checks," the stubby little man interjected, pudgy hands on broad hips. "And the chair was worth twenty dollars, at least. Cough it up, and I won't charge for the scratch he left on the bar."

Jeff reached into his pocket with his good hand and withdrew a small roll of bills. He handed it to Jilly. "Take what you need."

When she'd paid the man who reminded her of a walking-talking cigar butt, she returned the bills to Jeff.

"Blake," she said to her teenage employee, handing him the keys, "take your father out to my car."

"Sure, Jilly. I don't know how to thank you for this. That guy called the sheriff, and if I get arrested or something, it could screw up my chances to go to college."

She didn't tell him that the sheriff probably hadn't been called. From what she remembered her stepdad saying, the sleazy proprietor had plenty of reasons to steer clear of law enforcement. "Well, you're going to live to tell about tonight, if you want."

Sneaking into Beauties and the Beat was a rite of passage for most boys in Rumor. At least, it had been when Jilly and Jeff were in high school. She doubted things had changed.

The cigar-chomping proprietor shoved the money into the front pocket of a brown polyester polo shirt that stretched tight across his belly, then nodded toward Blake's staggering dad. "That SOB a friend of yours?"

Jilly didn't bother to answer his question. "I'd like a receipt, please."

"A receipt? You gotta be kiddin' me. How 'bout that guy gets out of here without me bashing his head in?"

Jeff took Jilly's arm. "Let's go."

"But—"

"But nothing. You don't need a receipt."

He took a step closer to the heavyset little man and narrowed his eyes. "This incident is over. And I suggest you forget any of us were here."

The little man laughed. "'Fraid your reputations can't hold up to a little talk?"

"For a guy who doesn't mind serving drinks to minors, I'd say you have the most to lose. Of course, closing down this dive would do the entire community a favor."

Then Jeff led Jilly out of the den of iniquity and across the graveled lot.

Again he'd stepped in as her hero, her knight in shining armor.

Now, there was a guy who was real husband and daddy material. Too bad he didn't have any plans to settle down and be part of a family.

Hers or anyone's.

Feeling a sharp pang of regret, she followed Jeff to the car, where Blake and his loser dad waited in the back seat.

Jeff slipped into the passenger seat, as Jilly took the keys from the kid.

"I'm really sorry about this," Blake said again.

Jeff didn't doubt that he was. He shot a glance at the drunk slouched in the back of Jilly's car and cursed under his breath. He wanted to give the guy a piece of his mind, but he figured it would be a waste of time.

"Don't worry about it," Jilly told the teen. "I'm glad we could help."

After formally introducing Jeff to Blake, the young man who someday wanted to be a pilot said, "Gosh, Mr. Forsythe, it's cool to meet you. I just wish it wasn't under such embarrassing circumstances."

"These things happen. Don't give it another thought." Jeff tried to brush off the incident as inconsequential, yet he doubted anyone in the car—other than the drunk who slumped against the window—believed it.

Jilly turned in her seat to address Blake. "I thought you told me your dad had to work. What happened?"

"He did, I think. But when I got home, he was gone. Then about an hour ago he called wanting a ride home from the strip joint. I guess one of his barroom buddies took him for a drink before work, but once my dad gets started, he doesn't know how to stop."

"What happened to the tire on your car?" Jeff asked the kid.

"I don't know. My dad's a mean drunk, and I think someone got pissed and sliced my tire to get even with him." The boy blew out a frustrated sigh. "Every time I manage to get some money saved, something like this happens."

Jilly turned in her seat. "I can give you an advance, then take a little bit out of your check each week until you pay me back."

And that would be how long? Jeff wondered. A year or two? He took another quick look in the rearview mirror, spotting the subdued troublemaker, his eyes closed, his mouth hanging open.

Surely, Jilly wouldn't keep paying the tab for a guy like that. The florist shop might be doing well, but he doubted she could afford to bail out her part-time employee's dad on a regular basis.

As they drew near the place where Jilly had grown up, the headlights illuminated the rusted tin structure. Someone else lived there now. And they'd hauled off the old car and mowed down the weeds.

He glanced across the seat and saw Jilly's gaze locked on the trailer house.

What did she see?

He wasn't entirely sure, but figured there was nothing he could do to erase her thoughts or lift her mood. Still, he was determined to try.

They dropped Blake and his father off at the apartment complex on Main Street, then returned to Jilly's house.

"You're awfully quiet," Jeff said as they entered the living room.

She looked at him with eyes that shimmered like melted chocolate, then shrugged.

"Hey, you're not going to get all soft and mushy on me, are you?" he asked.

"It's not my style, I know. But I guess my hormones are going whacky."

He slipped his arm around her, pulled her close. It seemed like such a natural thing to do. "I wish I could do something to help, but this pregnancy thing is out of my league."

"Mine, too," she admitted.

"Maybe you need to focus on the baby." He really didn't know how *that* idea had popped out, but he figured those maternal instincts and urges should kick in and help her through all this.

"You're probably right."

He decided to help her along, jumpstart those instincts and urges. "Do you want a boy or a girl?"

"I just want the baby to be healthy. And happy. It really doesn't matter."

So much for that. Well, Jeff wasn't a quitter. He'd give the ol' jumpstart one more try. "Maybe we should go shopping on Saturday, pick up some things for the baby at MonMart."

"Ah, Jeff," she said, turning into him and circling

her arms around his waist. She laid her head against his chest and sent his heartbeat into overdrive. "You're so good to me. And you always know the right things to say and do."

Knowing what to say right now had been a crap-shoot. What the hell did he know about expectant mothers or babies? He'd just pulled the shopping idea out of his hat.

He rested his cheek against the silky strands of her hair, savored holding her in his arms. So soft, so gentle.

Just as he was beginning to think a guy could get used to her embrace, she pulled back, stepped away, leaving a gaping hole between them. "I'd like to go to MonMart on Saturday. I think getting ready for the baby is a good idea."

"Great. And then we'll go to dinner on Saturday night, to celebrate."

She smiled, revealing the chipped-tooth grin he adored. "I haven't been out to dinner in months."

Since Cain, he realized, but he didn't point it out, hoping her grief would burn itself out. And he couldn't think of a better way to shed the past than to look forward to the future, to focus on making the best of a difficult situation.

"How about we have a special dinner, downstairs at the Rooftop Café?" He tossed her a smile.

And she shot it right back. "I love their desserts. And since I'm eating for two now—"

"That's the spirit." Jeff chuckled. "Then it's settled."

She nodded, but something told him things were still very much up in the air.

The Rooftop Café was packed on Saturday night, and Jeff was glad he'd made reservations.

"This way, please," the hostess said, as she led them to a table by the window.

More than a few heads turned as they entered, but Jeff didn't give it much thought. His broken arm had drawn attention from the entire community, especially today while shopping at MonMart with Jilly.

He'd insisted she choose some maternity clothes, as well as the little gowns and bootees that she enjoyed picking out. The shopping trip, he'd quickly decided, had been a great idea, and it only validated the wisdom of the surprise he had up his sleeve.

He held out Jilly's chair, and she flashed him that smile he loved to see.

They'd only studied the menu for a minute or two when she excused herself to go to the ladies's room. "If the waiter comes by, will you order me a cup of tea?"

"Sure."

Jilly hadn't been gone for more than a minute when Mrs. Evans, his old Sunday school teacher, made her way to the table.

"Jeffrey, I want you to know that I received the

darling invitation to Jilly's baby shower. Where did you find something so cute?"

Jeff glanced toward the doorway that led to the rest rooms before responding. He wouldn't address the elderly woman's question about where he'd found the darling invitations.

Shoot, he didn't even know what they looked like since his cousin Maura had picked them out and mailed them. But as the host, his name was on it. And he'd come up with the guest list. "I hope you can join us, Mrs. Evans."

She placed a liver-spotted hand upon her chest. "Why, of course I'm coming, Jeffrey. I love baby showers!"

Jeff didn't know the first thing about showers, but with Maura's enthusiastic response to his plea for help, he'd figured they might as well invite most of the community. It was one way to show Jilly his support.

Maura had told him, since the baby wasn't due for months, it was a bit early to throw a shower. But since he'd be long gone before Jilly's time got close, it was fine.

Some folks could be gossipy, especially in Rumor, but with the Kingsley and Forsythe names on the invitation, he doubted people would find much fault at all with Jilly's situation.

Jeff glanced at the doorway and, not spotting Jilly yet, placed a finger against his mouth. "Shh. It's a *surprise*."

"I know that, dear. You don't need to worry about me spilling the beans." She beamed with pride. "And everyone thinks it's so cute—a man planning a baby shower. And heartwarming, too."

Yeah, well, he didn't think it was particularly cute. And Maura, fortunately, was doing most of the work and making him look good. "Thank you, Mrs. Evans."

"I didn't know Jilly was expecting," the woman said. "And I've yet to meet her husband."

Whether Mrs. Evans was tactfully trying to ask questions, Jeff didn't know. He'd told Maura that Cain had fathered the baby, but he wasn't sure what Jilly intended to tell the people of Rumor. So he steered clear of the elderly woman's comment.

"By the way," Mrs. Evans said, bending closer. "The girls in my knitting group are thrilled that you invited us. Just you wait and see what we come up with as gifts."

Jeff glanced toward the doorway again, spotting Jilly as she flashed him a smile and closed in on their conversation. "Here she comes."

Would the sweet, little old lady get the hint and keep quiet?

"Hello, Mrs. Evans," Jilly said upon her return.

"Good evening, dear. I wanted to tell you those flowers at Mildred's memorial service were just lovely."

"Thank you." Jilly took her seat. "I knew how much Mrs. Sanderson loved carnations."

"That she surely did." Mrs. Evans smiled a little too gaily to be thinking about carnations or memorial services for poor, departed Mildred. "Well, Jeffrey, I'll leave you two children to chat." Then she shuffled off to join her friends.

When they were alone, Jeff reached across the linen-draped table and took Jilly's hand.

"You look pretty tonight," he said, wanting Jilly to feel good about herself, appreciated.

"Thank you." She tilted her head to the side, as though surprised at his comment. "You've never said anything like that to me before."

He hadn't. Not because she wasn't attractive, though. They were friends—good friends who'd been through a lot together. Her looks had never mattered.

But they mattered tonight.

Red highlights in her hair—highlights he'd never noticed before—glistened in the candlelight.

And talk about healthy glows, the hormones were doing a real number on her complexion. Or had she always had that sparkle?

If so, why was it stimulating his pulse now?

He stopped staring at her, choosing to look at the candles, the crystal vase of flowers on the table.

That was it. The romantic ambience was creating havoc with his determination to keep things platonic and on an even keel.

Just in time to diffuse Jeff's unwelcome thoughts,

the waiter strolled over to their table. "Are you ready to order?"

"I am." Jilly looked at Jeff, eyes bright and alluring. "I'm hungry. How about you?"

"Yeah. Me, too," he said, struggling with another kind of hunger.

And an unsettling attraction to his best friend—his pregnant best friend.

A vulnerable young woman who needed a hell of a lot more than a footloose pilot could provide.

# *Chapter Seven*

A memorial service for Cain was held at the Rumor Community Church on Monday afternoon.

The white clapboard house of worship had filled early with people wanting to pay their last respects to the Rumor fireman who'd died in the blaze that still burned out of control.

Flowers lined the altar, and a closed casket sat solemnly on display.

It all seemed so surreal, not just Cain's death or the service, but the entire relationship Jilly'd had with the fireman.

She sat in the third pew, Jeff at her side. More than once, she had to take a tissue from the wad she'd crammed into her purse. And each time her complex emotions gave way to tears, Jeff would squeeze her hand, letting her know he cared.

What would she have done without Jeff in her life?

What would she do when he left for his home in Colorado?

When the hymns had been sung and the scripture had been read, the minister spoke of life after death. Then he provided time for the mourners to speak. Several in the church took the opportunity.

Reed Kingsley spoke of Cain's sense of duty, of his dedication to protecting the community. Another fireman, Dave Colton, told of Cain's penchant for practical jokes and his love for the ladies.

Jilly sat through it all, her tumbled emotions playing havoc with her conscience. She felt saddened by Cain's death, but not like she suspected a grieving lover should. He'd broken her heart months ago, and she was over him in a romantic sense, even though a part of him and their relationship would live on in her child.

What haunted her, driving a spike into her conscience, was the fact she didn't feel much of anything else. Just the same generic sadness she would have felt if anyone else in the community had passed away.

Anyone but Jeff.

Losing her best friend would devastate her, and she shuddered at the thought.

Pastor Rayburn, a tall, gangly man who reminded her of a fatherly, gray-haired Ichabod Crane, stood at the dark-oak pulpit that had held the notes of numerous ministers over the years. "Would anyone else care to speak, to share a memory of Cain Kincaid? We have time for one more."

Jilly didn't know why she did it, didn't know why she stood. And she sure as heck didn't know what she would say, but she pulled her hand from Jeff's grasp and made her way to the front of the church.

Her heart tumbled in her chest, and she feared her words wouldn't form. But she stood before the people of Rumor, the people she'd so hoped would accept her as a respected part of them.

"I—" She cleared her throat and started over. "Cain and I dated a while back. Some of you knew that."

A few heads nodded, and Jilly spotted a smile or two, which helped her tongue to loosen, the words to flow.

"Several days before his death, I learned that I… that he and I…were expecting a baby."

Murmurs filled the small church, and Jilly gripped the pulpit, held tight to the hand-carved oak that had stood solid in the Rumor Community Church for years, through baptisms, weddings and funerals, through the tears of celebration and sorrow.

"I told Cain about the baby, just before he went out to fight the fire."

And he laughed at me, questioned the baby's paternity. The cruel memory blazed bright, but she kept the pain to herself.

His cruel implication that she might have cheated on him had pierced her to the quick.

But Cain had also regrouped, she reminded herself. He'd said that he needed time to think.

Deep in her heart Jilly had to believe that he would have accepted the child eventually.

"Cain and I didn't get a chance to discuss the future, thinking that we had a lifetime ahead of us to make plans." She glanced at Jeff, hoping to draw strength from his watchful eyes, his sturdy presence, his supportive smile. "I hope those of you who are here today in remembrance and respect for Cain Kincaid will show that same concern for his child, as it grows up in Rumor without the benefit of a father."

Then she stepped away from the pulpit and returned to her seat.

Pastor Rayburn thanked those who had spoken for sharing their memories, then asked the congregation to join with him and sing hymn 247, "Amazing Grace."

Mrs. Evans, who sat at the organ, began to play the familiar tune, and the congregation broke into song.

One woman in the row behind Jilly sang louder than the others, and the words rang clear, soothing Jilly in a way no one ever had.

"I once was lost, but now am found, was blind but now I see."

Jilly closed her eyes and let the words sweep over her, giving her the first sense of peace she'd had in years.

God, it seemed, had forgiven and accepted her. She hoped the people of Rumor would, too.

"'Tis grace that brought me safe thus far and grace will lead me home."

Four days later Jilly stood over her worktable, creating a floral arrangement the president of the hospital board would send to Carolyn Kingsley in appreciation for her help on the last fund-raiser.

After inserting a white orchid, she stood back and gave the work a careful appraisal. Not bad, if she did say so herself. Mrs. Kingsley would be pleased when Blake delivered it to the ranch later this afternoon.

Jeff had offered to take it himself, but Jilly refused to consider the idea. "The flowers will mean more to her if Blake drives up in the delivery van and takes them to her door."

"Whatever you say." Jeff brushed a kiss on her brow, then wished her a great day. "I'll pick up dinner from the Calico Diner and a movie. How does that sound to you?"

"Good."

It sounded great, actually. Jilly could grow used to going home to Jeff, to having dinner with him, to sharing their days with each other.

*Too* used to it.

More often than not she found it hard to keep her eyes off him, and even harder to keep her hands from reaching out, stroking his cheek, lifting her mouth for a kiss that would prove much hotter than the sweet, brotherly blessings he'd been prone to place on her brow lately.

She scolded herself for thinking of Jeff in a sexual way. He was her oldest and dearest friend, and she would soon be as sexy as a chenille housecoat. What had gotten into her?

She laid the blame on the hormones that had invaded her body and her life, yet the problem was that her friendship with Jeff had deepened, whether she wanted to admit it or not. And she feared that her pregnancy had nothing to do with myriad feelings battering her heart.

Leaving Mrs. Kingsley's arrangement on the worktable, Jilly took the bucket of water that had once held flowers outside to empty.

The morning sun burned brightly, and birds chirped from the treetops in the empty field across the way. She dumped the water, then, noticing movement in the trees, paused on the porch.

Michael Cantrell, teenage son of the rich software mogul who lived in the mansion across the field from her shop, stood by himself, waving his arms and moving his lips.

Jilly didn't see anyone nearby. Who was the kid talking to? Himself? Maybe he was practicing for a school play.

Rumor gossips said the kid was a bit odd, much like his uncle Guy. "Too smart and scientific for the likes of us," one old man had said.

Jilly didn't think anyone could be too smart. But

Michael's strange behavior drew her attention. She glanced at the sun that had moved high in the sky. School was still in session. Was he playing hooky?

Her curiosity was definitely piqued, particularly since his aunt, Wanda Cantrell, had been found dead with Morris Templeton, and his uncle Guy, the high school science teacher, had disappeared. Maybe stress had caused the kid to lose it.

Of course, there was that wild tale she'd heard the other day at the drugstore. Someone said that Guy claimed to be invisible. Maybe the teenager was trying to perpetuate the story by playacting and hoping some gullible person would buy the science teacher's weird claim.

If Jilly weren't so busy, she'd ease closer, try to figure out what the kid was doing.

As it was, she stood rooted to the spot like a snoopy old woman with nothing better to do.

Fourteen-year-old Michael Cantrell placed his hands on his hips, while studying the shadows in the trees. His uncle had called him on his cell phone and asked that he meet him just beyond the trees that surrounded the Cantrell estate on which Michael and his dad lived.

Michael had to skip school in order to do so. His uncle was a real stickler for education, but he was also absentminded enough to forget what day of the week it was.

His uncle's request was odd because no one had

seen him since before the science fair and the fire. But Michael would have done anything for the man he respected. He and Unk were close, much closer than Michael was to his dad.

"Okay, I'm here, Unk. But stop messing with me. Come out where I can see you."

"I'm merely steps away from you, Michael. I'm invisible."

"Yeah, right. And I'm the Wizard of Oz."

Twigs snapped, the sound growing closer. Still Michael couldn't see him. He'd heard a rumor at school that his uncle had claimed to be invisible, but he'd merely shrugged it off. There was all kinds of crazy speculation about the man's disappearance and the evidence found on Logan's Hill that suggested he'd been at the scene either before or after Aunt Wanda and Morris Templeton had died.

Unk's presence seemed to close in on Michael, and he picked up a scent of that cheap aftershave his uncle favored.

Was it possible? Could Unk be invisible? No way. Guy Cantrell might be a scientific whiz, but he was also a clever magician and used science to wow the kids in class.

"I know this is hard to believe," Guy's voice said. "But I can explain."

Michael furrowed his brow, skeptical, but growing more impressed by the minute. This was one heck of a practical joke. How'd he do it? Electronic device? A speaker? "Go ahead, I'm listening."

Someone touched Michael's shoulder, yet no one was there. He jumped back, nearly tripping over a pinecone and falling on his butt.

"Are you okay?" Guy Cantrell took a step forward, wanting to pull his nephew to his feet. But he didn't want to frighten the boy, especially when he was desperate for Michael's help.

"What's the trick?" Michael asked, scrambling to his feet and tugging on the waistband of his baggy pants.

"There's no trick. I'm really invisible. But I don't blame you for being skeptical. Linda Fioretti…I mean Ms. Fioretti…or would that be Mrs. Kingsley now?" Guy scratched his head, trying to remember professional protocol when talking to his nephew about a fellow teacher at the high school.

"It's Kingsley," Michael corrected.

"That's right." Guy knew people in town thought of him as an absentminded professor, but brilliant minds moved along at light-speed, sometimes scattering less important thoughts by the wayside. "Linda married Tag, if I remember correctly."

"What about Mrs. Kingsley?" Michael asked.

"She didn't believe me. But it's the truth, Michael. I'm not pulling your leg."

Michael stepped forward, reached out his hands and gave Guy's shoulder and chest a firm pat-down. "Wow," was all the kid could say.

"You remember how we were working on that formula to heal scars?"

Michael nodded, eyes still wide and bewildered, but his bright mind no doubt zipping and zapping right along.

"Well, it's a long story, but heat must have been the missing ingredient in my formula. It not only healed my scars; it made my skin completely translucent."

A broad smile settled on Michael's face. "That's amazing, Unk. Just think of the money you can make selling that to the CIA. You'll be famous."

It was great to see Michael's enthusiasm return. The boy had always had an adventurous spirit, but since his mother's desertion when he was four, he also carried a chip on his shoulder.

Guy chuckled. "Not so fast, son. The formula still has some problems, and I've got a lot of work to do."

"What can I do to help?"

"I need my notes from the lab in my garage so I can figure out what happened and how to fix it," Guy explained. "But the police have my house under surveillance, and I don't know when—or if—I'll become visible again."

The boy smiled, bright blue eyes glimmering with self-confidence. "You can count on me."

Guy placed his hands upon the boy's narrow shoulders. "Now be careful. You're going to have to sneak in after dark. And I hear that there's a community party in the works Saturday afternoon. People will be distracted, so you might have a better chance if you try to sneak into my place after dark on Saturday."

"You're not talking to a kid," Michael said. "You can depend on me."

Guy slowly shook his head, glad Michael couldn't see the apprehension on his face.

Something told Guy he had a lot more to worry about than becoming visible and perfecting his formula.

Still standing on the back porch of the florist shop, Jilly continued to study Michael Cantrell a while longer, in spite of the floral orders that awaited her attention.

"What are you doing?"

Jeff's voice caught her off guard, and she dropped the empty bucket she'd been holding.

Feeling like a Peeping Tom and not any better than some of the gossipy old ladies she'd often complained about, Jilly stooped to pick up the empty bucket and conjured a smile to hide her guilt. "I'm just pouring out some dirty water. What are you doing?"

"Not much. But I'm getting cabin fever."

"You're outside," she reminded him.

Had he grown tired of being in Rumor? Was he ready to spread his wings and fly? The thought of him leaving in the next day or two didn't sit well, but there wasn't anything she could do about it.

Jeff took the bucket from her hand. "Can you take a break?"

Not really, she wanted to say. She had several orders yet to fill, or else she'd have to come in super early tomorrow morning. But how many days would Jeff remain in town? How many more times would she have the opportunity to take a break with him?

"Would an hour be enough?"

"No," he said, flashing her a gorgeous smile. "But I'll make it work."

"What have you got in mind?"

"Let's drive out to the landing field, look at the planes."

Just like old times, Jilly thought. Going out to the small airport had been his favorite thing to do when they were both teenagers. She couldn't begin to count the days they'd gone out to the airstrip to talk to pilots and watch planes take off and land.

She smiled. "Let me put the Out To Lunch sign on the door and I'll be ready."

Minutes later they drove out of town.

Jeff didn't know why he asked Jilly to ride with him. He certainly could have gone alone, gotten his fix of takeoffs and landings by himself. But it felt right to have Jilly at his side, as it had in the past.

He didn't suppose she got any real thrill out of seeing the planes, talking to the guys who hung out at the airport. Maybe it just made him happy to know she cared enough to humor him. As it was, he was glad to give her a break from her busy day.

He slid a glance across the seat, saw her scanning

the skyline and smiled. "Did you ever come out here? After I left town?"

"Do you want to know the truth?"

He nodded.

"Sometimes, when I wanted a friend and had no one in sight, I'd come out here and feel close to you." She offered him a silly grin. "Weird, huh?"

Weird? No it was touching, almost to the point of being heart wrenching.

Jilly deserved a ton of friends, but she'd never gone the extra mile, never liked stepping out to make a friend on her own. He figured she didn't trust most people to accept her for herself.

Maybe the baby shower would draw her into the community. And, speaking of the shower, he still needed to figure out a way to get her to the party without blowing the surprise.

"I went out to the ranch this morning, after dropping you off for work." He didn't tell her that he and Maura went over plans for the shower. Or that he'd preferred chocolate cake rather than white with that lemony, mango-and-passion-fruit filling Maura insisted upon ordering. "Aunt Carolyn wants me to invite you to lunch tomorrow. I know you usually work on Saturday, but can you make it?"

"She's including me for lunch?"

Jeff nodded. "She wants to offer you her support. She's always had a soft spot for babies and pregnant women."

He didn't tell her that his aunt had been moved

during Jilly's announcement at the funeral services and was pleased to host the shower in the gardens of her home.

Jilly placed a hand on her expanding tummy, caressed the swell where her baby grew. "I guess I can make it. But I've been closing down my shop a lot lately. I hope it doesn't cost me any customers."

"You have the only florist shop in town, Jilly. Not that you should take advantage of the fact, but it won't hurt you to take an hour or two off, here and there."

Like she had today.

To be with him.

He slid her another glance. He hoped his aunt wasn't the only person in the community to feel sympathetic toward an unwed mother who could use a friend, someone to lean on when Jeff left town.

And he would leave—as soon as Jilly was feeling better about the future and he was cleared to fly. Hopefully, the fire would be out by then, but if not, he'd be part of the fire-fighting squadron again.

As they approached the airstrip, saw the wind sock flying in the air, a red-and-white Cessna ready to take off, Jeff felt the familiar thrill of flight, the sense of freedom he always missed while on the ground.

"You love this place, don't you?" Jilly asked, her brown eyes watching him, seeing the inner man more clearly than anyone else ever had. And even though he'd kept his feelings close to the vest, it didn't bother him that Jilly saw through him.

He nodded. "You've got that right. I love air-fields, planes, jets and choppers. It's not this place in particular."

At least he hadn't thought there was anything out of the ordinary about this place. But standing here, at the first airstrip he'd ever seen, with Jilly at his side, something warm and special washed over him.

He slid a glance at her, realizing she made this place special. And memorable.

God, she was pretty in that yellow sundress that reminded him of springtime and buttercups. She had a fresh, earthy glow about her, and a smile that could light up a room.

A man would be damn lucky to have Jilly as a wife.

For a moment the idea of marriage and picket fences slipped into view, but he swept the thought away as briskly as he would cobwebs in the attic. Jilly was rooted in their hometown, just as surely as the flowers with which she worked each day.

And Jeff had been born to fly, to soar. To live unfettered and free.

He opened the door, and she followed suit. As they strode toward the hangar, a Queensland heeler bounded toward them, ears perked, tail wagging, barking to beat the band.

"How you doing, Spice?"

The dog seemed to recognize him and slowed his run.

"You sure that's Spice?" she asked, nodding toward

the dog. "I never could remember which one was Sugar and which one was Spice."

"Sugar is the black lab," Jeff said. "And the female."

The elderly widow who lived down the road from the airstrip had two dogs that found the planes and activity far more interesting than a run-down yard, especially when the fence was too old to keep mending. When she passed away, the man who owned the airstrip, Lee Henderson, started feeding them. It appeared the dogs lived here now. Or at least one of them did.

Jeff patted Spice's head, taking time to rub its ears. "Lose your friend?"

"How sad," Jilly said.

Jeff thought about telling her that dogs didn't have friends, but something told him Jilly would disagree, and he'd be hard-pressed to argue. It sure seemed as if Sugar and Spice had been friends.

"Oh, look," Jilly said. "There's Sugar."

The dog wandered out of the hangar, her belly boasting a passel of unborn pups. He supposed Sugar and Spice were more than friends, and smiled.

As they walked to the chain-link fence that surrounded the airfield and protected parked planes, a yellow Piper Cub was entering the pattern to land.

"That's the first plane I learned to fly," Jeff said.

"That particular one?"

"No. One just like it." His thoughts drifted back

to the early days, to the time when a boy's dreams had come true.

She slipped her hand into his good one, and he gave it a squeeze.

What was with all the hand holding they were doing lately? He could have found an excuse to pull free, maybe grab hold of the wire fence, but he didn't.

For some reason it felt right to hold her hand, to keep her near.

The pilot of the Piper cut his approach short, and came in too fast and too high.

Jeff shook his head and mumbled, "Beginner."

Jilly laughed, then gave his hand a tug. Not hard but enough to cause him to turn, to catch sight of the sunlight dancing in her hair, the glimmer of the gold flecks in her rich, brown eyes, the light scattering of freckles across her nose.

The enticing way her smile disappeared and her lips parted…inviting him to close in on her, place his mouth on hers, give her the kind of kiss that stoked a fire in a man's blood.

An overwhelming flood of desire swept through him, demanding that he pull her close, lose himself in her kiss.

He only needed to lower his head, lift her chin and let himself go.

And he almost did, almost gave in to temptation and the promise of passion.

Almost.

But not quite.

Instead he turned to watch the Piper taxi to a stop, his heart pounding hard, insistent.

But for the life of him, he wasn't going to kiss Jilly like that. Wasn't going to leave them both wondering where their friendship had gone.

Or what the future held.

## *Chapter Eight*

Jeff and Jilly drove through the impressive iron gates that marked the entrance of the Kingsley Ranch.

The estate on the family's vast cattle ranch had always impressed Jilly to the point of intimidation, but she shoved her nervousness aside. Carolyn Kingsley certainly wouldn't have invited her to lunch if she hadn't meant it as a gesture of kindness and acceptance.

Jilly parked the car in the circular drive, then stole a glance in the rearview mirror to check her hair, her lipstick.

Jeff laughed. "Come on. You look great. Don't be nervous."

"I'm not," Jilly said, although she was, just a bit. She studied the house, a chateau-like log structure that stood three stories high, logs bolstered by stones, rooftops boasting steeples.

She blew out a sigh. Imagine that, little Jilly Davis, lunching with the rich and famous, or so it seemed.

"It's no big deal," Jeff said. "Just a lunch."

"You were born to live in this kind of grandeur, and I wasn't. It's a big deal to me."

He took her hand, as he'd done so many times during the past couple of weeks in an outward sign of intimacy, yet he still managed to maintain a friendly distance.

At the airfield she'd seen passion brewing in his eyes and had felt a similar desire herself. She could have sworn he was going to kiss her that day, and not one of those brotherly little smacks on the cheek or brow.

But he hadn't kissed her. And she wasn't sure whether she was disappointed or not.

Scratch that; she'd been disappointed, all right. Why lie to herself? She'd wanted that kiss so badly she could taste it. In fact, just thinking about kissing Jeff made her imagination run wild.

As they entered the marble-tiled foyer, Carolyn greeted both Jeff and Jilly with a hug. It seemed so natural, yet so surreal.

Those old feelings of insecurity put up a desperate fight for survival. Jilly hadn't had many occasions to visit the Kingsley Ranch, but not because Jeff hadn't wanted to take her home. Rather, the house and people were far more elegant than she was used to. In the past she'd felt uncomfortable with an invitation to visit, and had found one excuse or another to decline. But today Carolyn made her feel truly welcome.

"I'm so glad you could join us, Jilly." The tall, auburn-haired socialite smiled warmly, then turned to Jeff. "Dear, why don't you show her to the patio. We're having lunch outside today, but I need to check on something in the kitchen."

"Sure." Jeff placed a hand on Jilly's shoulder and guided her through the spacious house.

"I can't believe you grew up in a place like this," Jilly whispered, as she took in the elegant beige-and-white decor, the original artwork on the walls, the sculptures that had undoubtedly cost a small fortune.

When they neared the expansive glass doorway that led to the lush gardens in the yard, his hand slipped to her back, and he said, "After you."

Jilly stepped onto the porch to a chorus of shouts. "Surprise!"

Her breath caught, and she could scarcely believe what she saw.

People. Tons of people. Smiling faces. Linen draped tables. Tissue-stuffed gift bags and colorfully wrapped presents.

"What is this?" she asked Jeff, sure someone had made a terrible mistake. Neither of them had a birthday anytime soon.

"Surprised?" he asked, sky-blue eyes glowing with pride.

That was an understatement. Jilly was floored and

not at all sure what to do, what to say. She stood silent, like one of the naked stone statues in the parklike yard, until she could ask, "What's the occasion?"

"It's a baby shower."

Her knees grew weak, and she reached for Jeff's good arm. "For me?"

"Most of Rumor has come together to welcome your baby. I take it that you're surprised."

Too stunned to speak, Jilly nodded. Somehow, a belated yes popped out of her mouth.

People began to greet her. Russell and Susannah Kingsley were first.

"Congratulations, Jilly." Susannah held her newly adopted baby on her hip. Not long ago, she and Russell had brought the dark-haired little girl home from China. "Babies are so precious."

The pretty redhead fairly glowed, which wasn't at all surprising since she'd recently announced her own pregnancy.

"Thank you, Susannah. And congratulations to you, too." Jilly touched Mei's little hand. One day she would hold her own child and count each finger and toe.

Tag and Linda Kingsley were next, their four-year-old daughter, Samantha, standing between them. Even Dr. Holmes and her husband, Devlin, had been invited.

Jeff and Jilly made the rounds, greeting everyone and accepting their best wishes.

"Where's Maura?" Jilly asked, surprised she

hadn't spotted Jeff's younger cousin and the Kingsleys' only daughter.

"She's on duty with the forest service this weekend. There was no way she could get out of it, not with the fire still burning out of control. She was really disappointed she couldn't be here but said she'd be thinking happy thoughts for you today." Jeff tugged at the collar of his white polo shirt. "I'm thirsty. Can I get you a glass of punch?"

"Yes. Please."

As Jeff walked away, Jilly scanned the verdant grounds and flower gardens that had gained the Kingsleys several photo spreads and articles in various home and garden magazines.

Across the way, standing in the shadow of a shade tree and steps away from the water fountain, she spotted a face from the past.

Ash McDonough, her old neighbor.

She hadn't seen him in years, not since he'd messed up his life—big-time—and let his sister, Emmy, down in the process.

Jilly supposed Ash had let her down, as well. She'd always looked up to him and his brother, Karl.

When Mom McDonough died of cancer, custody of Emmy fell to the older boys, but Karl, who'd gone to the Gulf War, hadn't returned, and Ash had gotten into trouble with the law. His conviction and subsequent prison term had left his younger sister to foster care.

As a result, Emmy was carted off to live with a family in Big Timber.

Since Jilly'd been a young teen without any means of transportation, the nearby town might as well have been Timbuktu, as far as she was concerned.

When the county social worker drove away with Emmy in her car, Jilly had cried herself sick. Never had she felt so alone. She'd been left without a place to escape her no-account mom and stepfather, no friend next door to tell her secrets to.

Jeff's friendship had always been special to her, but he hadn't been able to replace the girlfriend who'd lived only yards away.

Apparently Ash McDonough was out of prison and had paid his debt to society.

She made her way toward the Italian fountain where he stood unsmiling, hands clasped behind his back, tormented gray eyes reflecting his disappointments and pain.

Jilly wasn't at all sure what to say to him, especially here and now, so she settled for "How've you been?"

"I'm okay."

She doubted that was entirely true, but it was just as well that he didn't go into details. Just seeing Ash again was a painful reminder of Emmy's fate, and Jilly would rather not contemplate the suffering his conscience had gone through while behind bars.

The man had paid a big price, she suspected, just knowing he'd abandoned his sister and left her heartbroken and in the hands of the state.

The anger Jilly had harbored began to wane. "I didn't know you were back in Rumor."

"I'm working at the Holmes Ranch, thanks to Colby taking a chance and hiring an ex-con on parole."

She nodded, then glanced toward the others mingling near tables and carved-stone benches scattered throughout the lawn and gardens. "I didn't expect to see you here."

He shrugged. "I was torn about coming. But I want to start patching things up with people from my past."

Ash had a lot of patching to do, she figured, especially with his little sister. "Have you seen Emmy?"

A flash of pain crossed his features. "Not yet. I understand, though, that she's doing fine. Got her nursing degree in Kentucky when she was living with Karl, and has a good job at a twenty-four-hour clinic in Big Timber."

"I bet she'd like to hear from you."

He made a sound of doubt with his mouth. "Y'think?"

Looking out into the crowd, Jilly noticed a few people watching them. Furrowed brows and frowns suggested more than a few weren't pleased to see Ash.

She hadn't been pleased to see him, either, but he'd been good to her, prior to his arrest. And she appreciated his efforts to keep her and Emmy on the straight and narrow, even if he didn't take his own advice.

As Ash scanned the crowd, Jilly suspected he noted the same grim expressions she'd seen.

"I paid for a crime I didn't commit," he said. "Some folks won't ever believe that, and it will take time for people to trust me again. But it's important that people like you believe me."

Ash had always proclaimed his innocence, while admitting his naiveté for getting into the mess in the first place.

"I believe you," she said.

"Thanks." He nodded toward the others, toward the frowns, crossed arms and noses in the air. "It's obvious not everyone will be quick to forgive or forget."

"They will with time."

"Yeah, maybe so." Ash withdrew his hands from behind his back and held out a fluffy, gray, stuffed rabbit. "I got you something. For the baby."

Jilly took the bunny from him, fingered the soft fur and held it against her chest. "Thank you. It's really cute."

"It reminded me of Bambi's rabbit friend. I remembered how much you liked that movie."

She had. Mom McDonough had taken her, Emmy and the boys to the Dollar Day matinee in Whitehorn one Saturday afternoon, where they'd had popcorn and soda and sat way up front in the third row. It had been Jilly's first time in a movie theater, and the memory still burned bright.

"Thank you for remembering." She lifted a long, droopy ear and fingered the soft fur. "I'm sure the baby will like it."

Ash cracked slight smile. "For what it's worth, Tessa Holmes told me you were having a girl. Congratulations."

*A girl?* Jilly's hand caressed the gentle swell of her stomach. Everyone in town knew Colby's wife, Tessa, had psychic abilities. Was Jilly having a baby girl? A daughter?

Hair ribbons and dollies. Pink and ruffles. She suddenly wanted to give her little girl all the things she'd ever wished for as a child, all the things her family hadn't provided for her.

"Thanks for sharing what Tessa said. I hope she's right."

Ash chuckled. "Tessa's always right."

Jilly smiled. "That's nice to know. I'd love to have a daughter."

"You'll make a good mother, Jilly."

She appreciated his vote of confidence. "If so, it's because your mom set such a good example for me."

Ash nodded in solemn acknowledgment and shared grief, then blew out a sigh. "Well, I'd better get back to the ranch. I'm sure the atmosphere will become more festive after I leave."

He was probably right, but she hesitated to agree. "Give Emmy a call, Ash."

"I will—sometime soon." Then he excused himself.

"Thanks for coming." Jilly meant the words. Coming here hadn't been easy, and it pleased her that he cared enough to stop by anyway.

She stroked the soft fur of the gray bunny she would call Thumper, watching Ash saunter away, a chip on his shoulder and, undoubtedly, remorse in his heart.

Before Jeff could reach the crystal punch bowl, Stratton approached, placed a hand on his shoulder and drew him away from the linen-draped beverage table.

His uncle nodded toward Ash McDonough. "What's that guy doing here?"

"I didn't invite him in particular, if that's what you're asking. But he's part of the community and was welcome to show up. Besides, Ash and Jilly were once neighbors."

"Yeah, well I don't trust him. And I'm not pleased about having a guy like that around."

"He's done his time." Jeff remembered how Ash had once been a decent guy and a friend of Jilly's. "And he's never stopped proclaiming his innocence."

"The prisons are filled with innocent people, if you ask them and their lawyers." Stratton, his once-dark hair now mostly gray, had mellowed in recent years, but he still stood his ground, still guarded his family and his turf.

Jeff caught his uncle's eye. "I don't think you have to worry about Ash."

Stratton, who was semiretired but still very much in control of his dynasty, grumbled under his breath. "You've always had a soft spot for people with questionable backgrounds."

"I hope you're not referring to Jilly." Jeff had assumed the days of his aunt's and uncle's disapproval of their friendship were long over.

"No, I'm not talking about Jilly. Why look at what she's done for herself. The florist shop is doing well, from what I hear."

It was no secret that Stratton Kingsley had ways of finding out privileged information. Jeff hoped his uncle hadn't been checking up on her. "Have you been talking to your friends at the bank?"

Stratton laughed. "Come on, Jeff. I see that delivery van of hers all over town. She's got to be doing well."

Maybe so, but Jeff still wouldn't put it past his uncle to talk to the banker and ask a few questions— just to appease his curiosity.

He wondered if Stratton suspected that Jeff had been the one to fund the loan she'd needed to open Jilly's Lilies. He supposed it didn't matter. Stratton might be curious, but that's as far as it would go. Besides, he wouldn't butt into Jeff's affairs or dealings.

Jeff gazed at Jilly, who stood near the fountain, her white cotton dress showing off a golden tan, the sunlight dancing on red highlights in her hair. She almost had a celestial glow, reminding him of an angel.

All right, maybe an angel with a tilted halo, but an angel just the same.

"You're gawking, boy."

Jeff looked at his uncle and saw the broad smile on his face. "What are you talking about?"

"Your aunt and I always figured there was more to your friendship than met the eye."

"There isn't," Jeff said. "Jilly's like a sister to me."

"You weren't looking at her that way."

Jeff rolled his eyes and shook his head, hoping to discourage his uncle from the truth. "She looks pretty in white. That's all."

"Yeah," Stratton said. "Pretty as a bride at an outdoor wedding."

"It's a baby shower," Jeff reminded him. "And there's nothing between us, other than childhood memories and mutual respect."

Stratton chuckled. "It's your story, Jeff. Tell it any way you like."

Jeff clicked his tongue. "I live in Colorado, for cripe's sake. And I might be on disability, but I'm tied to the Forestry Service and MAFFS. I've got places to go, things to do. I don't plan on marrying anyone, at least for a long time."

"Family is important."

"I know that. And I have a family."

"Yes, but I'm talking about you having a wife and kids someday."

"Maybe someday," Jeff said to appease his uncle, who not only adored the two granddaughters he had, but hoped to welcome many more children into the fold.

As loving as his aunt, uncle and cousins had been, Jeff had never really felt as though he fit into the Kingsley family. He'd always thought of himself as an outsider looking in. And that was fine with him.

There were fewer requirements that way, fewer commitments. He came home for the holidays—on occasion—which seemed to please everyone. A wife and children would expect more of his time than an occasional Thanksgiving, Christmas or Easter.

This conversation was veering into a subject Jeff no longer wanted to discuss. "I told Jilly I'd get her some punch, Uncle Stratton. So if you'll excuse me?"

"Sure. But one last thing, Jeff. We all miss you. Why don't you give settling down some thought?"

"Clip my wings?" Jeff asked, stepping away from his uncle and heading back to the punch bowl. "No, thank you. I like things just the way they are."

As Jeff waited for a silver-haired woman who worked for the caterer to fill two glasses, he listened to Linda, Tag's wife, speak to a woman he suspected was another schoolteacher. "Guy Cantrell called me a couple weeks ago and claimed to be invisible."

"You've got to be kidding," the teacher said. "Guy has always had a high-tech mind, but surely he doesn't think people will believe that."

Jeff wanted to laugh at the ridiculous notion, but pretended not to hear. He'd always thought the high-school science teacher was kind of weird. Maybe the mad scientist had finally gone off the deep end.

But with the police looking for him, Cantrell had better come up with something more plausible than that goofy tale. His partially burned backpack had been found near the bodies of his wife and Morris Templeton, and the police had plenty of questions to ask him—as soon as they found him.

When the silver-haired woman handed him the two glasses of punch he'd requested, Jeff returned to Jilly's side.

The happy smile she flashed him was worth a million bucks. Maybe more.

"Thanks, Jeff."

"You're welcome. Don't spill it on that pretty white dress."

She sent him another one of her chipped-tooth smiles. "I'm not talking about the punch, although I appreciated that, too. But I meant thank you for everything."

When she placed an angel-soft kiss on his cheek, her fresh floral scent lingered after she'd stepped away.

And so did the warm glow in his heart.

After a catered lunch of grilled chicken, rice pilaf and Greek salad, followed by a white cake with a tropical-fruit filling—the tastiest dessert she'd ever eaten—Jilly opened her many gifts amidst oohs and aahs.

She could scarcely believe the generosity of the community, as she received hand-knit baby blankets and matching booties, undershirts, sleepers. Where would she put the precious little things?

She'd planned to make the small bedroom next to hers a nursery, but it looked as though she'd have to buy a chest of drawers first—a chest that would be full in no time at all.

Just as she'd always hoped and dreamed, her baby would start life with everything new, unlike the hand-me-downs Jilly had worn from infancy to high school.

It was difficult not to feel excited about putting away each little gown, sleeper and outfit.

The blue funk she'd been in since finding out about the unplanned pregnancy began to lift. Her attitude brightened.

And Jeff, bless his heart, had set all this in motion.

She was having a baby. And everything was going to be okay.

No, it was better than okay. It was exciting and wonderful.

As the guests slowly left, and the caterers began to clear the tables, Jilly sat on a stone bench and watched Jeff as he talked to his uncle.

"Mind if I join you?" Carolyn Kingsley asked.

"Please do." Jilly made room, and Jeff's aunt took a seat.

"You received some lovely gifts."

"I sure did. Thank you for allowing Jeff to have the party here. Everything was perfect. And I'm going to get a lot of use out of that playpen you and Stratton gave me. I'll probably keep it at the shop so the baby can watch me while I work."

"You're welcome, dear. I'm glad the playpen will be useful. And as for having the party? It was a pleasure. Stratton and I were happy to help Jeff with the shower." She chuckled softly. "Jeff was so cute when he came up with the idea. I told him that it was a bit soon, but since he's not planning to be in town much longer, he wanted you to have the party now, while he could be here to share the day with you."

The thought of Jeff leaving struck a painful chord that went beyond disappointment, although she knew he'd leave soon. His arm was on the mend. But Jilly had gotten used to having him around, to passing him in the hall, watching him across the dinner table. Seeing him play with Posey as though he really liked the little dog he called Dust Mop.

"I'm sorry about your loss," Carolyn said. "Death is never easy."

Jilly nodded, sorry, too, but not for the reason most people would suspect. "It's sad that the baby won't know its father."

"You're right. But Cain really wasn't the right man for you. He was much too pretentious and bold."

"I know." Jilly looked at the dainty woman with auburn hair and warm blue eyes. "Jeff tried to warn me not to get involved with him, but I didn't listen. And he was right."

"The strongest love often grows where you least expect it," Carolyn said. "It's steadfast instead of flashy."

Was she talking about Jeff? Giving Jilly some kind of family approval? Had she seen something Jilly hadn't?

Jilly glanced at Jeff, saw the way he stood proud and tall. Watched him laugh at something his uncle said.

Their friendship had changed, that was for sure. It had deepened into another dimension.

She'd seen the way Jeff looked at her sometimes, when he thought she wasn't watching. He felt something, too.

Was it love? Or something darn close to it?

Jeff shot her a dazzling smile, and her heart skipped a beat. God help her, she was falling in love with her best friend, if she hadn't done so already.

What was she going to do about it?

Jilly might be able to win Jeff's love, but did she want to?

If she were selfish, the answer would be yes. But she desperately wanted stability for her baby—and for herself, too. At one time her life had been too unstable, but not anymore.

She liked living in Rumor where she had a thriving business and a mortgage on a house that was slowly becoming a home.

And Jeff loved flying, loved the adventures that took him away from home several days a week.

In order to make a relationship work, one of them would have to give up everything.

But Jilly refused to let that happen. She wasn't going to place herself or Jeff in the position of making choices and decisions like that. Her dreams meant too much to her.

And Jeff's dreams meant a great deal to her, too.

It seemed like a lose-lose situation, because in this case, winning would mean watching a loved one's dreams go up in smoke.

"I've always wanted Jeff to settle in Rumor," Carolyn said, "to build a home on the ranch, if he'd like to."

It was no secret that Carolyn Kingsley had loved her sister, Jackie Forsythe. For that reason, Jeff always held a special place in her heart. It was no wonder she wanted to have her nephew near.

"I think Jeff likes living in Colorado," Jilly said,

wishing as much as Carolyn did that he would stick around town.

"Maybe you can persuade him into moving home." Carolyn looked at her with such hope in her eyes that Jilly didn't know what to say.

The truth, she supposed would be her best bet. Jeff didn't want to settle down in Rumor, and having to do so would take the light out of his eyes. But Jilly decided a white lie would be easier to voice. "Maybe someday he'll move back home."

But she knew that was as likely as her sprouting wings.

# *Chapter Nine*

Jeff had to borrow one of the ranch pickups to haul Jilly's loot home from the shower, but her joyful expression made the entire project worthwhile.

His gift waited at her house on Lost Lane, hidden in the spare room she planned to use as a nursery. Jeff had struck a deal with the MonMart department manager to have a baby crib, mattress and matching chest of drawers delivered while they were at the shower.

As Jeff carried some of the larger items from the truck, Jilly took a batch of smaller gifts into the living room, then went to find her beloved Posey.

Jeff hated to admit it, but there was something about that scruffy little dog that he found entertaining. As he deposited another load of gifts near the fireplace, the goofy dog that was so ugly it was cute scurried into the room. When Posey saw Jeff, she gave a yappy bark of welcome. Apparently, she found something appealing about him, too.

Jeff couldn't help but chuckle. "Hey, Dust Mop. Better stay out of the way, or someone's going to step on you."

He and Jilly made several trips to the truck until the gifts littered the living room. When they'd placed the last of the presents on the carpeted floor, Jilly kicked off her sandals.

She placed her hands on her hips and surveyed the stacks and overflowing boxes of gifts. Her eyes glimmered, appreciation evident. "Can you believe this?"

"Looks like you're off to a good start, Jilly. That baby won't be lacking much." Other than a father, of course, but he let the words remain unspoken.

She eased closer to him and wrapped her arms around his neck. "Thanks again, Jeff."

Her scent filled his lungs, and her breasts pressed softly against his chest. He had the urge to nuzzle her neck, kiss the soft spot behind her ear.

*Whoa.* Not good. He backed away and tried to conjure an unaffected smile. "You're welcome. I was glad to do it."

He might have broken the embrace, but not the connection. Or the compulsion to gaze at her.

She stood in the center of the room in bare feet, the hem of her white dress teasing shapely calves, spaghetti straps revealing her neck and shoulders— the neck and shoulders he'd wanted to kiss.

Back off, he told himself. Break the mood. Do something.

"Look at you," Jeff said, offering a friendly smile when he wanted to offer so much more. "Barefoot and pregnant."

She glanced down and pressed her hands against her stomach. The white cotton of her dress outlined the bulge of her womb. "I'm getting awfully fat, aren't I?"

"No," he said, his voice huskier than he'd anticipated. "You look prettier than ever before."

And she did. Pregnancy looked good on her. Damn good.

He was struck with a compulsion to place a hand on the mound where her baby grew, caress both mother and child. Again he shrugged off the urge.

"By the way," he said, trying to weaken the hold she had over him. "I've got a gift for you, too."

"You do?"

"Yep. Come with me." He led her to the spare room where he expected to find the crib waiting.

What the heck?

There stood the white chest of drawers he'd picked out. And the mattress that was supposed to be top of the line. But the crib was still in a box.

If he'd known the crib he'd seen on display came unassembled, he'd have paid the delivery guys to set it up. As it was, he'd have to put the baby's bed together himself.

But how hard could that be?

Jilly ran a hand along the white dresser, then stooped to look at the picture of the crib on the rectangular box.

He hoped she liked the one he'd chosen. "I purchased it at MonMart and still have the receipt. If you want a different color or style, we can exchange it."

"It's just perfect." She threw her arms around his neck—again—and gave him a heady squeeze. "I love it."

"Good." He closed his eyes, briefly enjoying the feel of her body, the scent that had engrained itself in his memory, even when she wasn't near.

She released him first, which was a good thing. He was having a damn hard time breaking their physical contact lately.

"Why don't I put it together now," he said, hoping to distract his mind and keep his hands busy. "I've got tools in the truck."

Minutes later he returned with a toolbox, and Jilly helped him tear into the sealed, rectangular carton. He pulled out the railed sides, a metal frame, the head and footboards, plastic bags with screws and bolts. It looked as if everything was there.

"Are you going to be able to do that with one arm?" she asked.

It would be tough; that was for sure.

She flashed him a smile, then snatched the instruction sheet. "I guess this will have to be a joint effort."

It took less time than he expected to put the crib together, and before he knew it, Jilly was placing a sheet on the little mattress.

After adding a frilly white comforter, she plopped a droopy-eared, stuffed rabbit on top. "Tah-dah!"

It looked good.

And it felt even better to stand side by side and admire their handiwork.

Jilly leaned into him in a move that seemed so natural, so right, that he slipped his good arm around her. She looked up at him, and when their gazes met, a jolt of awareness shot through him. Unable to help himself, he bent to give her a friendly kiss.

But as soon as his lips touched hers, friendship flew by the wayside and something else took its place.

The kiss started sweetly, gently, but the passion that had lain dormant rose to the surface. And when Jilly opened her mouth, welcoming his tongue, he was lost.

As he discovered the wet velvety softness of her mouth, the cast on his arm didn't prohibit his good hand from exploring the gentle contours of her body. He pulled her flush against his growing arousal.

Their tongues mated in deep, vigorous hunger. A moan sounded low in her throat, and he was lost. Lost in a swirl of pounding blood and heat. Desire shot clean through him, urging him to take her to bed and make love to her all night long. Fast and furious. Slow and easy.

When was the last time a kiss had so quickly sent his pulse skyrocketing or his blood throbbing into a demanding erection?

He wanted to explore far more than her sleek, wet mouth, and that scared him senseless. Pulling away, he tried to break the frightening spell she'd cast on him.

"I'm sorry, Jilly. I don't know what got into me." He raked his good hand through his hair, as if the movement might clarify things in his mind.

It didn't.

"Whatever it was got into me, too," she said, offering him that chipped-tooth smile. A telltale flush had spread along her neck and chest, indicating she'd been as sexually aroused as he.

Kissing her like that had been stupid. Crazy. And he couldn't let it happen again. Before saying or doing something idiotic, like making promises he couldn't possibly keep or kissing her again, he struggled to come up with an excuse to leave.

This was one night he couldn't sleep at her house, knowing she was just down the hall.

He shoved his good hand into the pocket of his jeans. "I've got to go back to the ranch tonight. I promised my uncle I'd help him clean up after the party."

She nodded, but he had a feeling she didn't buy his excuse. The Kingsleys had hired help to handle cleanups. By now the ranch was completely back in order.

But here, in the confines of Jilly's small house, everything had been torn wide open and feelings had run amok, leaving things far from orderly. And he had no idea when his emotions would settle down, when everything would go back to normal. And that scared the hell out of him.

What had gotten into him, kissing Jilly like that? She needed a man who would set down roots and make a home in Rumor. A guy who would build a tire swing in the back yard, who'd putter around the garage on a Saturday afternoon. A guy who'd be content staying at home every night.

Jilly needed a family man.

And there was no way in the world Jeff was that guy.

Jilly watched Jeff climb into the pickup and drive away before she closed the door and locked down the house for the night.

As she wandered into the bedroom, she touched her fingers to her swollen lips and relived the first— and probably the last—real kiss she and Jeff had ever shared.

It had been fiery. Mind-boggling. And the sizzling arousal had sent her heart soaring. In fact, it had been so hot, so good, that it frightened her in many ways.

The scariest of all was Jeff's reaction, his obvious discomfort with the step they'd taken. He'd certainly backpedaled, hadn't he? And he couldn't seem to get away from her fast enough.

Her heart felt torn in two, and she feared she would never recover when he left town and went back to Denver for good. Tears welled up in her eyes, and she swiped at them with the back of her hand.

What was she going to do?

Before she could come up with an answer to the question, she heard a noise outside.

Footsteps?

Jilly strode to the window and stole a peek through the blinds. A dark figure sneaked past her yard and appeared to be going toward Guy Cantrell's house. A deputy maybe?

Ever since the fire, the discovery of Guy's backpack and the partially burned bodies of Wanda Cantrell and Morris Templeton, the sheriff had been looking for Guy and had his house under surveillance.

Nope. Not a police officer. Not with those baggy jeans, oversize shirt and backward baseball cap. And certainly not looking that sneaky and suspicious.

Guy maybe?

No. Not dressed like that—unless he was in disguise.

She flipped the switch that would illuminate her backyard and reveal the prowler. Well, what do you know?

Michael Cantrell.

What was Guy's teenage nephew doing? He was

obviously trying to avoid notice. Should she blow the whistle on him?

Or would the police find him without her involvement?

"Damn," Michael uttered when Unk's pretty neighbor turned on her porch light. He tried to duck into the shadows and hide. Normally he could have walked down his own long driveway, then crossed the street to his uncle's yard, but the cops had that place locked up tight.

It was just as well that his uncle suggested he wait until Saturday night to sneak in. It gave him the chance to watch the deputies who surrounded the yard, to check out their habits. Twenty-four hours had allowed him time to figure out a way to slip into the house.

When the deputy walking the perimeter of the yard started toward the front, Michael made his move, stealthily slipping across the lawn his uncle hadn't mowed in ages, then dashing to the back door.

He pulled out the key he'd been given years ago, back when he and his uncle began working together in the lab, then entered the house.

Whew. He'd have to use the Braille method to find his way from the kitchen to the lab where Unk kept the notebooks he needed.

A few minutes later, after banging his shin on a stool, Michael found the notebooks and slipped them into his backpack. If he got caught, he'd claim the notebooks were his and part of a science homework assignment.

If he got caught.

Shoot. He'd better think of a good excuse, a reason for being inside his uncle's house. He sure couldn't tell anyone the truth. They'd never believe him. Besides, he'd take Unk's secret to the grave if he had to.

And if his father found out what he was doing, Michael might see the inside of a grave sooner than he expected.

As he fumbled his way through the living room, his hands brushed against a small box on the end table.

His aunt Wanda's cigarettes.

Hey, Michael could always tell the police he'd sneaked over here to have a smoke. He felt along the tabletop until he found a lighter. Alibi in hand, he headed for the back door.

Through the kitchen window he watched until the deputy circling the house moved to the front. When it was safe, he let himself out, the cigarettes and lighter in his hand.

Michael made it to the trees, pride in his clandestine accomplishment swelling his chest. Just in case he wasn't in the clear yet, he pulled out a cigarette and popped it in his mouth. His back to the house, he clicked the lighter.

It wasn't as though he wanted a cigarette. Heck,

he didn't even smoke. But it felt kind of like a cool thing to do.

"Stop!" a voice yelled at his back, as a high-beam flashlight lit his path to escape. "Stop or I'll shoot."

Michael's heart raced, and, lifting the hands that held the cigarettes and flickering lighter, he turned. A lit cigarette dangled from his mouth.

The deputy stood with gun raised and flashlight aimed at Michael's eyes. "What are you doing here, kid?"

Michael squinted and shrugged. "Just having a smoke." For effect, he inhaled like a hood.

Then coughed.

"Bronchitis," he uttered as an explanation. What was it about these dumb tobacco sticks that appealed to people?

"What's your name?" the officer asked.

"Michael Cantrell." He pulled the cigarette from his mouth. "I live across the street."

"Well, let's see what your dad says when I take you home."

Yeah, let's.

His dad was going to hit the roof. Well, so what? Their relationship had never been good anyway.

Moments later, they stood before the mansion where Michael and his dad lived in virtual reality, with every electronic game and toy imaginable. The only one who kept them both grounded was Bently— former tutor and family friend.

"Maaaan," the deputy said, drawing out the word and his reaction. "Some place you have here."

When Bently answered the door, he glanced first at the officer, then at Michael. "What seems to be the problem?"

"I need to talk to Max Cantrell. Is he here?"

"Please come inside." Bently flashed Michael one of those proper English what-have-you-done-this-time looks.

Well, he'd find out soon enough. There'd be hell to pay, he supposed. But it was worth it. He'd gotten the notebooks Uncle Guy needed.

His father entered the room, a stern expression on his face. "What's going on?"

"Mr. Cantrell, I caught your boy loitering around an off-limits area that's under surveillance. And," the deputy said, "he was smoking."

If looks could kill, Michael was heading for the graveyard.

"Smoking?" His dad looked at him as though he was a juvenile delinquent.

Michael merely shrugged, which only caused his dad's lips to tighten and his facial muscles to tense.

"Are you taking him to juvenile hall?" Max asked the deputy. The frustration evident in the tone of the paternal voice suggested he might welcome the idea of Michael having a sleepover in juvie.

"No, sir. I just wanted to escort him home, make sure you knew what he was up to."

Max crossed his arms. "Go to your room. I'll be there in a minute."

As Michael headed upstairs, he heard his dad mumble under his breath—something about the woes of a single parent.

Yeah, well Michael wasn't too happy about his lot in life, either.

Long after the deputy had led Michael Cantrell away, Jilly stood at the window and peered into the darkness. She'd seen the boy light up a cigarette and figured the officer had taken him home. Home to his dad.

Max Cantrell had more money than Fort Knox, but it wasn't enough to ensure his son stayed home and kept out of trouble.

Suddenly, parenting seemed like a much bigger, much scarier job than Jilly had expected.

Posey barked and jumped at her feet, begging for attention.

She picked up the dog and pushed the scraggly brown hair from its face to reveal big brown eyes full of love. "Looks like it'll be you and me raising this baby, Posey."

The little dog flicked a warm tongue across her nose, offering support and understanding.

Jilly had a business, which equated to income. And she had a house that was fast becoming a home. And a nursery. A crib, a chest of drawers. Baby clothes.

Posey licked her nose again, as if reminding Jilly they had love to offer the baby.

Could a loving mother compensate a child for not having a father? She hoped so.

Jilly would do whatever it took to be the best single parent alive, but the fact that Jeff had taken off like a thief in the night worried her.

What if things had gotten too heavy between them, too uncomfortable? What if Jeff decided he didn't want to maintain their friendship, even at a distance?

Jilly might do all right as a single mom.

But how would she fare without Jeff?

## Chapter Ten

Jilly hadn't seen Jeff since the night of the shower. And as the second day dawned without even a phone call, disappointment and sorrow nearly ripped her apart.

She figured he was running scared after that kiss, and if it hadn't curled her toes, too, she'd think his spooked reaction was funny.

But there wasn't anything funny about what she was feeling or what was happening to their friendship. She'd fallen in love with her best friend, and the earth-spinning kiss had only sealed her sorry fate.

It didn't take a brain surgeon to figure out that Jeff had dashed out of her house with his tail between his legs. The kiss had scared him, and probably for more reasons than the obvious.

When he finally walked into Jilly's Lilies, wearing faded jeans, a black T-shirt and a sheepish expression, her heart skipped a beat, excitement surged and she nearly dropped the bucket full of white chrysanthemums she carried in her arms. But her self-esteem wouldn't allow her to show signs of vulnerability.

Determined to salvage their friendship, as well as her pride, she set the bucket on the floor, leaned against the worktable and crossed her arms. "Feeling better?"

He furrowed his brow. "What are you talking about?"

Was he afraid she'd try to wangle a commitment out of him? Fat chance of that.

Jeff had never dated one woman at a time. He didn't make promises like that. Of course, he wasn't a jerk about it, either. As his best friend, she knew that for a fact.

More than a few girls had cried on Jilly's shoulder about his honesty. According to Jenny Parker, one of the girls he liked in high school, Jeff had asked her out by saying, "I'm dating two or three girls right now. I'd like to date you, too."

Jenny had hoped to win his heart, as well as his high school ring, but she'd crashed and burned.

Jilly clicked her tongue. "That kiss we shared turned you inside out, flyboy, and you're still recovering."

He scanned the small shop—looking for eavesdroppers, she assumed.

Crossing her arms, she shifted her weight to one foot. "The coast is clear. It's just you and me."

"Come on, Jilly. Settle down. I apologized to you for that."

"For what?"

"Taking advantage of you."

"Oh, for crying out loud." She plopped a hand down on the worktable in exasperation. "I'm an unwed mother, for goodness' sake. Do you think one little kiss is going hurt me? Isn't that like closing the barn door after the cow ran out?"

"I'm not talking about taking advantage of you sexually. I'm worried about the emotional stuff."

She knew exactly what he was talking about. Her emotions had been topsy-turvy ever since he came back to town, but she wouldn't let him off the hook. She supposed it was a man/woman, Mars/Venus sort of thing, but she wanted to hear him say it, to have him admit his feelings—whatever they were.

He might not love her in the way she'd fallen for him, but he was definitely feeling something other than friendship. "What kind of emotional stuff are you talking about?"

He raked a hand through his hair. "When you kissed me like that—"

"What do you mean, when *I* kissed *you?* Don't accuse me of trying to put the moves on you. Admit it. You wanted that kiss as badly as I did."

"Okay. So we both got a little carried away. Getting physically involved could really mess up our friendship."

"It was a simple kiss."

"The hell it was." Anger, frustration and guilt appeared to war for the right of expression on his face.

As his best friend, she should probably be more sensitive to his discomfort, but her lips curled in a smile. "If it wasn't a simple kiss, then what was it?"

"It was—" He paused and studied her with a furrowed brow. "What did you think it was?"

"I thought it was just a little sexual experimentation. That's all. We were both curious. And now we know."

"Now we know what?"

"That sex would be out of this world, if we were inclined to wander down that path."

"That's the wrong way for us to wander."

"You're right," she said, wanting to regain the upper hand, stay on top. Fight for emotional survival. "And it's over. No big deal." She nodded toward the refrigerator case that lined the back wall. "Would you bring me that container of yellow roses?"

"Sure," Jeff said, glad for a chore and to be off the hook. He felt like a real jerk for bailing out on her, but it was his own conscience that had him on edge. He'd lost his head when he kissed her, not to mention his balance. And that scared him spitless.

He wasn't a love-'em-and-leave-'em kind of guy, but neither was he the kind to make promises he couldn't keep. Especially to the best friend he'd ever had.

All he needed was to have Jilly fall for him, in a romantic sense. She would expect him to stick around town, to be part of the community. But that wasn't going to happen.

From the day Aunt Carolyn had brought him home, the day of his mother's funeral, he'd felt out of place. Sure, his aunt and uncle had tried to make him feel at home, suggesting he call them mom and dad and referring to Russell, Tag and Reed as brothers and to Maura as his sister.

But Jeff had held firm to the familial boundaries and official titles. He was a nephew and cousin of the Kingsleys. Nothing more, nothing less.

He'd had a wonderful mother, Jaclyn Forsythe, a beautiful woman who loved her son as much as she did the jet-setting world into which she'd been born.

Refusing to shake the Forsythe name and become a Kingsley had been the only way he could hang on to his mother, to her memory and to the love they had for each other in spite of her footloose and sometimes wild life-style.

Like his mother, Jeff had been born a free spirit. Settling down, conforming to community and family life would only shackle him, make him feel wounded and broken.

He placed the container of flowers on Jilly's work-table, watched as she created a floral arrangement as though the hot kiss they'd shared had never happened, as though it hadn't affected her the way it had him.

She'd been right. The kiss had turned him inside out, and he hadn't recovered yet. Maybe he never would.

No other woman had ever affected him like that, unbalanced him, made him yearn for things he'd never wanted before.

He watched her move, watched her create a work of art from a bucket of flowers and greenery, fingers deftly working.

Her silky brown hair brushed against her shoulder when she cocked her head to study the slowly emerging floral masterpiece. Her mouth opened slightly, and she brushed the tip of her tongue across her top lip.

How could she look so damn sexy without even trying?

"Hey," he said.

She looked up, brown eyes snaring him into a sweet, chocolaty depth. "What?"

"Are you mad?"

"Mad?" she asked. "At you? For ducking out and disappearing like I had the pox? Whatever made you think a thing like that?"

Okay, she was steaming. And he deserved it. But this wasn't the kind of thing he found easy to talk about.

He blew out the breath he hadn't known he'd been holding. "All right, Jilly. That kiss scared the hell out of me."

She stepped away from the worktable and crossed her arms, eyes tempting him like two Hershey kisses. "No one knows you like I do, Jeff. I understand your love of flying, your need for freedom. And even if I were crazy in love with you, I wouldn't expect anything from you other than friendship."

That was good. Wasn't it?

Before he could respond, she added, "I hope you won't allow that kiss—as hot as it was—to ruin what we have. I'd like to keep you in my life."

"I've forgotten it already," he lied. Then he gave her a hug to prove he wasn't going to let the kiss affect him.

Trouble was, it already had.

Far more than he was willing to admit.

He held his breath, refused to breathe in her scent, refused to think about her breasts splayed against his chest.

Desperate to ignore the feel of her in his arms and the growing sense of lust in his blood, he mentally recited the Declaration of Independence—at least the lines he could still remember.

Trouble was, when he got to the part about the pursuit of happiness, his resolve flew out the window.

"See how easy that was?" she asked as she stepped away, out of his arms.

"Yeah."

But it hadn't been easy.

His arms hung at his sides, limp and empty. He watched as Jilly went back to work as though neither the other night's kiss or today's hug had bothered her in the least.

But for some reason, he suspected she might be faking it. Jilly was tough on the outside, but on the inside she was a softy. And more vulnerable than she'd ever admit. She needed someone to look out for her and the baby.

For a moment he was struck with the urge to propose, to offer her and the baby his name.

But how could he even consider something like that? That would make him a family man, something he'd never wanted to be.

His career as a pilot suited him fine. He enjoyed being on call, packing up at a moment's notice and flying off to places unknown. Being a husband and father would change everything.

"What do you think?" Jilly asked.

About what? Marrying her? Being grounded in Rumor? Tying his hopes and dreams to a picket fence?

She nodded toward the floral arrangement. "Do you think this is too sparse?"

"Maybe you should add another yellow rose or two. I think it needs more color."

She smiled, revealing the chipped tooth she'd

earned in first grade. He loved that smile, and he feared that he loved her, too. Maybe he'd always loved her.

But marriage?

There had to be another way he could help and support his best friend. The community that offered her roots and stability would only tie him down.

The bell over the florist shop door chimed, as Blake and a pretty redheaded girl walked in. Grateful for the interruption, Jeff greeted the kid who worked after school and on weekends for Jilly.

"I want you guys to meet a friend of mine," Blake said, "Sheree Henry."

"I'm glad he finally brought you by," Jilly told the young girl.

Blake turned a deep shade of pink, causing Jeff to wonder if the two teens were merely friends or more than that.

"Sheree and I are on the dance committee," Blake said. "At the end of summer, the junior- and senior-class officers host the back to school dance to help welcome all the new freshmen to Rumor High."

Jeff remembered the annual event, although he and Jilly had never been part of the committee to plan the dance. But they'd both gone and had a lot of fun. "Where is it being held?"

"In the MonMart parking lot. We're looking for chaperones and thought you guys would be cool, since you're so young."

Jilly laughed. "Sounds like fun. I'll help chaperone." She flashed Jeff a smile. "How about you, flyboy?"

"When is it?" Jeff asked.

"Next Saturday night," Sheree said. "We've already got a few adults to agree, including Susannah and Russell Kingsley. But we need two more."

At the mention of Russell's name, Jeff frowned. With a recent business acquisition that took plenty of time, not to mention a new wife and baby, his oldest Kingsley cousin was a busy man. "How'd you get Russell to agree to chaperone the high school dance?"

"Sheree is a friend of the Kingsleys and works at Rumor Rugrats, the nursery school Susannah owns. She just asked, and they both said okay."

"So how about it?" Jilly looked at Jeff. "Are you going to help me chaperone?"

"Sure. Why not?" Jeff chuckled. "You have a way of dragging me along on your adventures."

"Life would be boring without me, wouldn't it?"

That was for sure. Jilly kept him on his toes. "It's a good thing I don't live in town."

Her face dropped, but only momentarily, and she quickly recovered her smile. "You're probably right about that. But don't worry, you'll be leaving soon."

Yes, he would. Now that Jilly appeared to have her life in order.

But why did his life feel out of whack?

\* \* \*

Jeff and Russell patrolled the perimeter of the dance, a sectioned-off part of the MonMart parking lot that had been barricaded with bales of hay and decorated with balloons and crepe paper.

Chinese lanterns cast a warm glow on the high-school kids, and a DJ played an array of hit songs.

"It's good to have you back in town," his older cousin and MonMart mogul said. "I'll bet Jilly appreciates having you around, too."

Jeff shot a glance at his best friend, who, along with Susannah Kingsley, chatted with Dee Dee Reingard. Jilly rested a hand on the swell of her growing belly, then laughed at something Dee Dee had said.

"Jilly's been through a lot." Jeff didn't mention Cain's death, but he didn't feel he had to. "I'm glad I could be here these past few weeks."

"Too bad you won't be here when the baby is born."

Jeff stiffened and slowed his pace. "Jilly knows I'm leaving. Are you suggesting I take on a responsibility that isn't mine?" His tone came out harsher than he anticipated, since the thought of stepping to the plate for his friend had continued to cross his mind.

"Hey, Jeff. I'm not suggesting anything of the kind." Russell placed a hand on his shoulder. "I imagine childbirth is tough enough for a woman to bear, even when she has someone to hold her hand."

The thought of Jilly in pain shot a dagger through Jeff's heart. Not only was the father of her baby dead, but she didn't have a mother or sister to be with her through labor and deliver.

She only had a friend.

*Him.*

Well, maybe he could come back for the baby's birth. That would be the right thing to do, the supportive thing to do.

He stole another glance at Jilly, saw her walk across the dance floor, avoiding bee-bopping teens along the way. She stopped near the large, blue plastic buckets of ice that held cans of soda, then gazed out into the dark of the night.

Looking for him?

How could someone appear so alone in a crowd?

She'd spent enough time in her life living on the edge of town—an outsider, more or less. Seeing her like that, apart from the community, was too much of a reminder of where she'd been, where she'd never belonged.

"Excuse me," he said to his cousin. "I'm going to ask a friend to dance."

Jeff made his way through the throng of teenage dancers and to the hay bale where Jilly stood.

When she spotted him, she smiled. "Have you busted anyone for smoking or drinking yet?"

Jeff laughed. "No. But I found a guy and a girl making out near a burned-out streetlamp in the parking lot."

She smiled. "And?"

"I told them they'd better join the dance before one of the other chaperones found them."

"And did they listen?"

He scanned the dance floor and spotted the couple moving to a slow song. "As a matter of fact, they did." He nodded toward Blake and Sheree who danced together, their affection for each other obvious, yet tasteful.

Jilly smiled wistfully. "They look good together, don't they?"

Jeff supposed they did. "They're just kids. They've got a lot of life ahead of them."

She nodded. "You're right, but Blake's had his share of misery in the past. I'm just glad he's found someone who cares about him."

Jeff didn't know Blake well, but that episode at Beauties and the Beat with his old man was enough to convince him the kid's life had been rough and would probably only get worse, unless Blake's father had a major attitude adjustment and made some big changes. From what Jeff had seen so far, it didn't seem likely, and he sympathized with the kid.

He figured that was the reason Jilly, whose own life had been one disappointment after another, had taken the kid under her wing. She probably understood the importance of having someone in her corner, if not in her world, more than anyone.

He slipped an arm around her and pulled her close. "Want to dance?"

"With you?" she asked, brow arching as though the idea had come out of the blue. A crooked grin suggested the question hadn't surprised her at all.

"Yeah. With me."

He led his friend out onto the dance floor, and against better judgment, pulled her close, inhaled her fresh floral scent, felt her softness meld with him.

Under a canopy of stars they swayed to the music, hearts beating in time.

"We never danced together in high school. Seems kind of funny now, doesn't it?"

Funny? No.

Surreal, maybe. And nice. A guy could get used to holding a woman like Jilly.

*Too* used to it.

But Jeff wouldn't worry about that now. Not while he had her in his arms. He'd be leaving soon enough, and this dance, this night would merely be a memory. For a brief moment he thought about never letting her go.

He closed his eyes, listened to the words of a love song and swayed to the mellow beat, Jilly in his arms, the peach scent of her shampoo taunting him.

All too soon the song ended. He released her with reluctance, but his gaze remained fixed on her.

As she turned to go, she swayed unsteadily on her feet. Had he not been close, not been watching, she might have fallen.

He grabbed her by the hand. "Are you okay?"

"Just a little light-headed, I guess." She offered him a smile. "Don't worry about me."

But he was worried. More than he should be. And more than she would ever know.

# *Chapter Eleven*

On Monday, as Jilly prepared to leave for an early-morning doctor's appointment, Jeff sat on the easy chair with Posey curled up in his lap.

It tickled her to see the tough guy soften toward the little dog, who for some reason adored Jeff and followed his every step. Posey had even begun to eagerly respond to the silly nickname of Dust Mop.

Jilly supposed she and the dog would both miss Jeff when he left. She had no idea when he'd be going, but the day was coming. She could feel it.

After the high school dance, he'd gone back home with her, but kept a respectable distance. Posey was the only one who received any affection, and more than once Jilly'd been tempted to jump into Jeff's lap and coax a reaction out of him.

But she hadn't. She respected him and his feelings too much.

So far, ignoring the fact he would soon head back to Colorado worked for her. It was, she supposed, a Scarlet O'Hara solution, but she wasn't going to think about the future until it rose up and slapped her in the face.

"Well, I'm off." She flashed a wistful smile at the man who would never be more to her than a friend. "You guys behave while I'm gone."

"Don't worry about us," Jeff said. "But be sure and tell the doctor about that dizzy stuff."

Jilly snatched her purse from the dining room table and slipped the strap over her shoulder. "What dizzy stuff?"

"Saturday night. After we danced, you were light-headed."

Yes, she remembered. But that wasn't from pregnancy. She had melted into Jeff's embrace, held him close and let herself pretend they were crazy in love. Dancing with him had left her weak-kneed, and when he'd stepped away, she'd nearly collapsed in a bone-less heap.

"I'm sure it was nothing," she said, unwilling for him to know the truth.

"Maybe not, but you'd better mention it, just to be on the safe side."

"Okay."

"And ask about whether you should be on your feet all day long," he added. "I think you should be taking it easy."

Jilly shot him a smile. "You're such a worrywart. Why don't you come with me?"

"To the doctor?" He scrunched his nose. "I don't think so."

"Why not? The last time I went to see Dr. Holmes, there were a couple of guys who went in the exam room with pregnant women."

He seemed to ponder her statement, but not too long. "I'm not your husband."

She was painfully aware of that but laughed it off. "So? You're my friend."

He glanced down at his booted feet, and she wasn't sure if he was considering her request or trying to come up with an excuse that wouldn't disappoint her.

She tucked a strand of hair behind her ear. "Besides, I'm hoping you'll agree to be my daughter's godfather."

"Your daughter?" he asked. "What if the baby's a boy?"

She knew better than to mention Tessa Holmes had said the baby was a girl. Jeff wasn't one to take much stock in vibes, visions or predictions. He was too rational and realistic to even consider the possibility.

"I just have a feeling the baby is a girl," she said. "But either way, you haven't answered my question about being the baby's godfather."

"I guess so," he said. "If I can be a long-distance godfather."

She swallowed the lump in her throat and blinked back a tear. His leaving was never far from his mind. Nor hers. "Sure. You don't have to live in town. But I hope you'll come by and see her sometime, not just call on occasion and send a birthday gift."

"I can probably manage a few visits each year. Is that often enough?"

It wasn't anywhere near often enough, but she wouldn't ask for more than he was willing to give. She'd have to settle for him taking on the occasional role of godfather. Still, she couldn't help pushing just a little more. "Does a few visits mean three?"

"I can't make any promises because of my commitment to MAFFS, but I'll give it my best shot to come back to Rumor for more than the baby's birthday and Christmas."

Although pleased with his concessions, Jilly feared he was struggling internally with the commitment to visit regularly.

Jeff didn't take promises lightly, and his word was always as dependable as tomorrow's sunrise. If he said he'd come more often than two or three times a year, he'd do his best.

"So," she said, shrugging off his obvious apprehension, "since you're the baby's godfather, it's only natural that you'd be interested in going with me to the doctor."

He scrunched his face again, and she felt as though she was forcing a heaping tablespoon of cod liver oil down his throat.

"Don't be afraid."

"I'm not afraid," he said, but the look on his face suggested otherwise.

"Then come with me."

"Okay, maybe I will." He placed Posey on the floor and stood.

"Great," she said, surprised that she'd actually been able to change his mind…his time.

"Since I'm going to be leaving Rumor soon, I'd like to make sure you're okay and that you're doing everything you're supposed to."

Jilly knew she shouldn't encourage his participation in her life, continue the charade, make believe he loved her and was here to stay. But for once in this pregnancy, she wanted to pretend that someone else—someone who really mattered—cared about her and her baby.

Ten minutes later they pulled into the parking lot of the renovated white clapboard house that had been converted into the Rumor Family Clinic.

Several times Jeff nearly backed out and let Jilly go to the clinic alone. But the fact was, he wanted to assure himself she'd be all right when he left town. And if that meant asking her doctor a few questions, then that's what he would do.

As he and Jilly reached the front door, Dev Holmes walked out. Jeff figured the man had either dropped off his wife or come by to chat since Dr. Brynna Holmes was Jilly's doctor.

Jeff and Dev had first met at the airfield years ago. While they greeted each other, Jilly went inside and checked in at the front desk.

"How's it going, Dev?"

"Great." The tall, sandy-haired ranch foreman and amateur pilot shot him a grin that validated his words. He nodded toward Jeff's arm. "Heard you've been grounded."

"Yeah, but only for a while."

"Heading back to Colorado when they take that thing off your arm?"

"Yep," Jeff said, nodding. "I'm getting antsy, though. Can't wait to get back in the cockpit."

Dev chuckled. "If things get too rough, I'll take you up in one of my planes."

Both men shared a love of anything that had to do with aviation, so Jeff had no doubt Dev understood exactly how he felt. "I might take you up on the offer."

"Just give me a call." Dev adjusted his black Stetson. "Come by and take a look at the ultralight I'm building for our honeymoon trip to Kenya."

"I'd like to see it." Jeff flashed him a smile. "Sounds like you're keeping busy."

"That's for sure. When we get back, I'm starting an outfitting service out of Rumor."

"A business like that ought to do well around here, particularly with all the hunters and fishermen looking for remote spots."

"That's what I figured."

A red-haired woman who looked about ready to give birth on the spot pushed a stroller toward the entrance, and Jeff opened the door for her.

"Well, I'd better get going," Dev said.

"Me, too. Jilly wants me to go in for her appointment."

"You'd better not keep her waiting."

"You're right." Jeff shook the man's hand. "Good luck with your charter service."

"Thanks."

As Jeff entered the nearly full waiting room, he spotted Jilly in a chair by the corner, next to a potted fern. She thumbed through a woman's magazine, but he didn't think she was actually reading it.

When he sat beside her, she slid him a smile. "For a while I thought you might have hitchhiked home."

"I tried, but couldn't catch a ride." He snatched a *Sports Illustrated* from the table next to him and extended booted feet.

How had she talked him into this?

Nearly ten minutes later Jilly was called back to the exam room by a stocky, dark-haired nurse, and Jeff experienced a flood of apprehension.

How did a doctor examine a pregnant woman?

Suddenly feeling way out of his league, he balked. "Maybe I ought to sit here and wait."

"No way. You promised." Then she took his hand and led him back to no-man's-land.

First stop was the scale.

"Turn around," Jilly told him. "Don't look."

"For cripe's sake. If you didn't want me to see how much you weigh, you should have let me wait outside."

The heavyset nurse grinned from ear to ear, and Jilly merely swatted at his arm.

Minutes later they entered a cramped exam room with a clean, medicinal smell that reminded Jeff of his short stay at the hospital. His first inclination was to take the coward's way out. "I'm not going to fit in here. Maybe I should wait outside and give the doctor more room—"

"Nothing doing," Jilly said. "This will be painless."

Yeah. Right.

The nurse instructed him to take a seat, as Jilly perched on the edge of the paper-lined table. At least Jilly hadn't been asked to undress.

Her blood pressure was normal. Thank goodness. One less worry.

"Oops," Jilly said. "Jeff, can you hand me my purse?"

He did, and she withdrew a small plastic bottle. The nurse opened the lid and stuck a paper dipstick inside.

"Good," the dark-haired woman said, as she studied the color and compared it to a chart.

Jeff squirmed in his seat. He could be out that door in two steps, but he'd have to shove the nurse out of the way.

"Dr. Holmes will be in shortly," the brunette said, before leaving the room.

Now was his chance, but when he glanced at Jilly and saw those chocolaty eyes crinkled in pleasure, he remained in his chair.

"I really appreciate this, Jeff."

"Yeah, well you're going to owe me—big-time."

She laughed. "No problem."

When Dr. Holmes entered the room, the walls began to close in on them, and Jeff was again struck with the urge to escape.

The pretty blond doctor, Dev's wife, introduced herself to him, then asked Jilly how she'd been feeling.

In no time at all, Jeff's questions had been answered, and he was assured that Jilly and the baby were as healthy as could be expected.

He blew out a slow sigh of relief. He'd made it through the exam unscathed, but about the time he thought they'd be excused to leave, the doctor asked Jilly to lie down.

Uh-oh…

Again, Jeff was ready to make a gridiron dash out the door but remained in his seat.

Dr. Holmes rang a button and asked someone named Evelyn to bring in the ultrasound machine. Then she probed the expanding bulge of Jilly's stomach.

Jeff nearly told her to take it easy and not poke

so hard. Wasn't she afraid of hurting something? Or shaking something loose?

"The baby seems to be growing at a normal pace," Dr. Holmes said. Then she took a big white tube and squirted a clear gel right on Jilly's skin.

What the heck was that goop for?

*Whoosh, whoosh, whoosh* sounded over a little speaker the doctor held in her hand, and she looked at Jeff and smiled. "That's the baby's heartbeat."

His mouth dropped, and he couldn't mask his awe. "It sounds like a little choo-choo train."

When he glanced at Jilly and saw the tears in her eyes, his heart turned to mush. There really was a little baby growing inside of her.

The child—boy or girl—began to take on its own persona. From now on Jeff would be watching out for two of them—Jilly and the baby.

When the woman named Evelyn pushed a cart into the room, Dr. Holmes began the ultrasound. A moving black-and-white image of Jilly's baby formed on a small screen like magic.

Jeff sat transfixed as the doctor pointed out the baby's head and spine, but the picture soon became pretty clear to him. He watched as the baby put a little fist in its mouth.

"She's sucking her thumb," the doctor said.

"She?" Jeff asked. "How do you know the baby's a girl?"

"She doesn't seem to have the necessary equipment to indicate she's a boy."

"Oh." He glanced at Jilly, saw happiness radiating on her face, saw her eyes damp and glistening.

Jeff feared his own eyes were damp, too, as he watched the screen, amazed at the miracle growing in Jilly's womb.

A baby girl.

And he was going to be her godfather.

Suddenly, Jeff wanted to know what the child looked like. Would she have Jilly's silky brown hair? Jilly's chocolaty eyes?

Or would she look like some unknown grandparent stuck out on some obscure branch of the family tree?

Somehow, Cain's genetic contribution didn't seem to matter in the least. This little girl was Jilly's daughter.

And Jeff's godchild.

He made a vow right then and there. That precious little girl wouldn't lack for anything—at least financially.

Jeff would see to that.

Maybe, after the appointment and when he'd dropped Jilly off at the florist shop, he would mosey over to MonMart and buy his new goddaughter a little pink bike. And a baby doll.

Did girls like wagons? He couldn't imagine why not.

A big grin tugged at his lips. This godfather stuff might be a lot of fun.

Jilly was in for a big surprise when she got home this evening.

Jeff left Jilly at the florist shop to begin her day, then proceeded to MonMart, where he snagged a cart and pushed it through the store.

He brushed past shoppers, some meandering through the store as though in a trance, others rushing to and fro as if they were preparing for a chance to appear on *Supermarket Sweep*.

Where in the world did they stash the toys in this store?

He made his way past household items, sports gear and the automotive department, until he finally spotted the toy section and stopped before a display of baby dolls.

How did a guy know which one was best?

One doll talked, which he thought might be cool. Another ate mock baby food and drank a bottle. Should he get fancy and go with the ballerina who danced on her toes?

He put them all into his cart.

"Can I help you?" a woman wearing a MonMart vest asked. She glanced at the boxes in his cart.

"I want to buy some toys a little girl will like."

"How old is she?" the woman asked.

"She's just a baby now, but I don't live in town and won't always be around. I just want to make sure she has everything a little girl would ever want."

"Well, you've got a good start." The woman

scanned the shelves. "How much do you want to spend?"

"The sky's the limit."

"Well then," the clerk said, brightening. "I suppose we'll need another shopping cart."

"Maybe two more," he said with a grin.

If Russell knew Jeff was here, he'd probably insist upon giving him a family discount, but Jeff didn't expect any favors or special treatment. He'd pay the advertised price, just like everyone else.

The larger items—rainbow-colored climbing structures and a sandbox that looked like a pirate's ship—were displayed on a shelf above the aisles of toys.

"How about one of those little kitchens?" he asked. "Girls like that stuff, don't they?"

The clerk smiled. "My daughter sure loves hers. She's always cooking dinner and making me try her latest pretend dish."

"All right. I'll need a kitchen. And maybe one of those big walk-in playhouses? The kind that go in the backyard?"

"This is one lucky baby," the woman said.

He didn't know about that. The baby wasn't going to be too fortunate in the daddy department, but she'd be darn lucky to have a mom like Jilly. And Jeff intended to make sure she had everything else she needed.

As he continued to choose toys, including a pink tricycle with a white wicker basket on the handlebars, the clerk retrieved another cart to help him collect his purchases.

"It's too bad I don't work on commission," she said. "I could retire."

Jeff laughed. "I'm a shirttail relative of the Kingsleys. Maybe I can put a good word in for you. You've been a great help to me."

"Oh, you don't have to do that. I'm just doing my job." Then the woman flashed him a smile and winked. "Believe me, I'm having fun helping you spend your money."

It took seven carts to contain Jeff's smaller purchases, and his credit card took a good-size hit, but he was proud of his gifts.

He'd have to talk to the store manager about having the bulk of his items delivered to Jilly's house later that afternoon. And there was a darn good chance he'd be assembling some of the toys until well past midnight. But he didn't care.

Jeff couldn't wait to see the look on Jilly's face when she saw what he'd done.

She might think he was spoiling her baby, but he hoped the toys would compensate for the child not having a father around the house.

And he also hoped that his generosity would appease the growing sense of guilt he felt at leaving Jilly and the baby to fend for themselves.

## Chapter Twelve

Jilly entered the living room of her once uncluttered house and gasped.

Toys, dolls, boxes, brown packaging, plastic wrap, nuts and bolts, an open toolbox. The place looked like Santa's workshop on Christmas Eve.

"What's all this?" she asked.

Jeff looked up from his work, as he sat on the floor assembling a pink tricycle. "Stuff for the baby. Think she'll like it?"

He'd obviously gone shopping. "What did you do? Buy out a store?"

"No, but the toy department of MonMart definitely needs to restock their shelves."

Jilly plopped down on the sofa and stared at the toys and games, some of which her child wouldn't be able to play with for years. "This must have cost a fortune."

"Nothing's too good for my goddaughter." Jeff studied an instruction sheet, then locked a black wheel into place.

Although thrilled that he wanted the best for her baby, the entire scene was a bit overwhelming. "Where am I going to put all of this?"

Jeff glanced up from his work, a screwdriver in his hand. "I hadn't thought about that. Maybe you'll have to convert that third bedroom into a playroom."

Jilly slowly shook her head and laughed. "The poor little girl doesn't even have a name yet, but she's got a house full of toys and dolls."

"Speaking of names," Jeff said. "What are we going to call her?"

*We?*

The fact that Jeff had included himself in the choosing of her daughter's name pleased her. And so did his generosity and thoughtfulness, even if it was a little over the top.

"I hadn't given names much thought, but I suppose we should come up with something. Do you have any ideas?" Jilly glanced at Posey, who growled and snapped at a piece of cardboard packaging, then dragged it down the hall. "On second thought, maybe you'd better leave the name to me. I don't want her ending up with a nickname like Dust Mop."

"No, that name's been taken. But give me some time, I'll think of something just as suitable." Jeff's dazzling smile nearly knocked her off her feet.

Eyes the color of the Montana sky locked on hers,

piercing her heart and sending a jolt of heat to her tummy and warmth to her heart.

What would she do without Jeff around on a daily basis, without his teasing smile, his rock-hard sense of right and wrong?

Unable to dwell on his leaving, she held tight to the conversation at hand. "The baby should have a name to be proud of, something fit for royalty."

"Like Elizabeth? Or Victoria?"

"Maybe." Jilly pondered for a moment, then brightened. "How did your mother spell her name?"

"My mom?" Jeff asked. "J-a-c-l-y-n, but everyone called her Jackie."

"I like Jaclyn. What do you think? Would you mind if we named the baby after your mother?"

"Not at all," Jeff said, his voice sounding much deeper than usual.

Jilly wasn't sure why she'd suggested it. Was she trying to extend the charade and pretend that Jeff would be a part of their family, their lives, their home?

Or had she merely wanted to give the baby a name that had meaning for them both?

Jeff had only been six when his mother died in a tragic car accident while coming home from a party late one Saturday night. He'd been heartbroken, and had held on to his grief, not wanting to share it with his aunt and uncle. But early on he'd opened up to Jilly, telling her stories of the good times he'd had with an unconventional high-society mother who'd adored her only child.

Jilly had always found the anecdotes entertaining and envisioned Jackie Forsythe as a young Auntie Mame.

"You remind me of her," Jeff said.

A vision of Auntie Mame danced to life, and Jilly grinned. "I remind you of your mother?"

He nodded. "You used to have that same spirit of adventure, that same naughty streak."

"You mean like that time out at the lake?"

Jeff and his friends had gone fishing out at Lake Monet one warm August day. And Jilly, who'd gone on a picnic with the McDonoughs, had spied them while hiking with Emmy. When the boys returned to the shore, their clothing was nowhere to be found. And to this day, she'd refused to tell him what she'd done with all their stuff.

"That was one of many times, I suppose. You also were the ringleader of that stunt at the high school."

"Are you referring to that basketball game with Whitehorn?"

"That's the one." When the team had taken the school bus to the game in Whitehorn, they returned to find the inside of their cars stuffed full of wadded newspapers and blown-up balloons. "That little prank taught us to lock our vehicles."

Jilly caressed her tummy. "Well, looks like my wild days are over."

"You can't kick a vibrant streak like that, Jilly. It's in the blood."

Maybe he was right, although the thought of bloodlines and genetics was a bit disturbing.

Jilly had hoped to leave her family ties behind. But would they creep up on her and infiltrate her happy home when she least expected it? Would history repeat itself, in spite of her best efforts to break free and start fresh?

What did she *really* know about normal families and loving homes?

She'd only been five when her dad ran off. The shadowy image of a tall man with dark hair and a prickly beard had faded a long time ago, but not the memory of that last, late-night argument. She could still recall the cursing and accusations he'd hurled at her mom, the sound of exploding glass as a bottle of rum slammed against the television screen.

That night, when the sheriff who'd been called to settle a domestic disturbance arrived, Jilly's father told her to go back to bed.

She had, but it had taken forever to fall asleep. And when she woke up the next morning her daddy was gone.

Jilly still didn't know the actual details of the fight, since her mom took that secret to her grave. But she suspected her mother had never gotten over him leaving, which is what Jilly had always told herself.

While growing up, it had helped to believe her mother had pined after her first love, then tried to fill the gaping hole in her heart by bringing home a string of stepdads—some official, some not—to replace him.

Jilly had always thought her mom had chosen to use drugs and alcohol as a means of coping with a broken heart. But as an adult, looking back, Jilly wondered whether her mother's drug-and-alcohol problems had led to her father leaving.

Maybe not.

He'd left Jilly, too, never even taking time to say goodbye.

She blew out a long sigh. At least her mom was at peace now. Six years ago, and shortly before the end of her senior year, Jilly had come home to find her mom's lifeless body in bed, sprawled on top of rumpled, yellowed sheets. On the nightstand, a prescription bottle of Valium rested beside a plastic ashtray overflowing with cigarette butts and ashes, an empty glass and a jug of cheap wine.

Whether her mom had checked out intentionally or not, Jilly would never know for sure. But she'd found it best not to dwell on the possibility.

"Hey," Jeff said, setting down the screwdriver and joining her on the couch. "What's the matter?"

"Nothing."

He placed a hand on her knee and gave it a gentle squeeze. "Don't snowball me. I've been reading your expressions for too long. What's bothering you?"

"I'm just thinking about my mother."

Jeff slipped an arm around her shoulder and

pulled her close. "Your mom might not have won Mother of the Year, but at least she gave you a basis for comparison."

"You mean, I can be a good mom because I've had firsthand experience with a lousy mother?" Jilly slowly shook her head and smiled. "Leave it to you to find something positive in every situation."

"There's no use stewing about things that can't be helped."

"You're right." She laid her head against his shoulder and relished his support—emotional as well as physical.

They sat like that for a while, quiet and pensive. In no time at all her mood mellowed, and she found herself cloaked in his musky scent, enjoying the comfort and intimacy of his touch.

Is this what it would be like to have Jeff as a lover or husband? To have him close every day?

His presence grew overwhelming, and Jilly had a difficult time keeping her hands to herself, as well as her thoughts.

Did he feel it, too? The warmth? The awareness? The attraction?

How could he not?

She looked up and his gaze snagged hers, pulling her into the sky-blue depth.

Oh, yes. He felt it all right. No doubt about it.

Would he bail out, like he had when they'd kissed the night of the baby shower? Or would he acknowledge the desire that burned between them and promised a star-bursting climax?

She wanted to make a move, to let him know how badly she wanted him—in a physical sense. What would he do if she turned into his embrace, lifted her mouth to his?

If he pushed her away or took off at a dead run, the rejection would crush her.

But maybe he only needed a little nudge.

She'd give anything to know what he was thinking.

Jeff wanted to take Jilly in his arms and kiss her again. The damn attraction he felt was impossible to ignore. He struggled with feelings he couldn't quite understand. Sure, some of them were easy to peg—a deepening friendship and an unwelcome but heady desire. An urge to protect his best friend.

But something else was slowly rising to the surface. Something he refused to analyze.

Look at the tricycle, he told himself, the fireplace, the baby doll in the corner.

Yet his eyes remained on Jilly, the woman who made no secret of the desire brewing in her soul.

Forsythe, get up and find that bushy little dog. Do something. Anything but look at the pretty woman sitting beside you.

In spite of his best efforts, his brains completely deserted him, and he ached with need. When had he wanted another woman like this?

By some fluke of fate and sheer force of will, he

managed to hold on to his self-control, but just barely. He seemed to be battling something that was much stronger than his willpower.

But when she flashed him a smile, revealing that slightly chipped tooth—her badge of courage—pent-up desire exploded and Jeff was lost.

He slipped his arm around her, pulled her close. His lips sought hers, and when she opened her mouth, accepting his kiss, he moaned in both resignation and wild need.

The kiss deepened, as tongues mated and hands desperately ached to touch, to caress, to lay claim to new ground. A sense of urgency and a pounding erection demanded he not turn back.

It both scared and excited him, yet he didn't let go, didn't stop. Even his cast didn't slow either one of them down, although it made things a bit more awkward and they had to work around it.

He slid his hand under her soft cotton shirt, only to find her skin softer, silkier than the fabric. His fingers skimmed along her ribs until they reached a lacy bra that barely contained her breasts—or his curiosity. He palmed the soft mounds until she whimpered, then struggled with the front snap until she helped him release the lace binding and push it aside.

Her nipples hardened at his touch, but before he could get his fill, she slipped out of the blouse, revealing full breasts that ached to be kissed, laved. He took one in his mouth, and she sucked in a breath and whimpered.

There, on the living room sofa, they made out like two teenagers with the entire house to themselves. But it wasn't a teenage libido urging Jeff on; it was a fully mature, fully aroused dose of testosterone that demanded release.

His flagging sense of right and wrong made one last, inept effort to stop him, to not let things go any further than he could handle. But they'd already gone way too far for him to pull back. To think of anything other than making love to her all night long, fast and furious, then slow and deliberate.

How could a woman he'd always thought of as a sister have this kind of effect on him? He hadn't a clue, but at this point he could only hope that she wanted him as badly as he wanted her.

Jilly could hardly think, other than wanting to drag Jeff to her bed where they would have more room, but she feared he'd stop the mindless assault on her body. As it was, she couldn't get enough of him, and if they wound up on the floor in a slick, panting heap, it was all right with her. She wanted to feel him inside of her, wanted him to fill the ache that grew deep in her core.

A part of her feared he'd grow serious and show the restraint she'd come to expect from him, but she intended to do her best to make his mind take a back seat to passion. Something told her she'd only have this chance, this night to make love to him. And once would have to be enough.

Determined to stoke the fire that burned inside

of him, she nearly tore the buttons off his shirt to reveal his skin, to brush her mouth against his chest, to take a nipple between her teeth and tease him to distraction.

But her efforts only seemed to backfire on her. It was her own desire that burned bright and hot. She was wild with need. "Jeff, please. I want you."

For a moment she feared her words would land on him like a bucket of cold water, and he would pull away, realize what they were about to embark upon.

He did stop but continued to hold her close. His breath came in short pants against her hair. "Ah, Jilly, are you sure about this?"

"I'm sure. And don't worry. I won't expect more from you than you're willing to give. I'm not asking for anything other than tonight."

Jeff feared the repercussions of this one night would last for a long time, but somehow it didn't seem to matter, not here and not now. He'd deal with his regret later. Hopefully, Jilly wouldn't suffer any lingering remorse.

He'd had a few one-night stands in his life, but this was different. This was Jilly. And she deserved so much more than he could offer.

She placed a hand upon his cheek. "Make love to me, Jeff."

"I don't want you to be sorry about this later," he said.

She reached into his lap, stroked his hardened arousal. "I won't let either one of us be sorry."

Fears of remorse and regret flew by the wayside, and as much as he wanted to argue, to put up a fight, a demanding erection insisted otherwise. "Let's finish this in bed."

"Good idea." She tongued his nipple for good measure, then took him by the hand and led him to her bedroom.

He knew how Adam had felt when Eve handed him that apple. He was too darn hungry to resist temptation. With the heat pounding in his blood, everything she said made sense. What would one night hurt?

Maybe, he tried to convince himself, making love would get those sexual thoughts of her out of his system once and for all. Yet he feared he was only kidding himself.

She led him to the bed and slowly slipped off the shorts she'd been wearing, revealing lace panties and a rounded tummy. Instead of dousing his desire, the reality of her pregnancy only made her appear more womanly, more appealing.

He sucked in a breath as her knuckles skimmed his belly and her fingers worked to undo the snap of his jeans. Within minutes he'd shucked his clothes and held her in his arms, skin to skin. Heat to heat.

She was beautiful, breathtaking, and he couldn't wait to take her, even if he couldn't make her his forever.

"Are you sure?" he asked one more time, hoping

to absolve himself from feeling any morning-after remorse.

"I want you more than I ever thought possible." She sat on the bed and lifted her arms to him, inviting him to join her.

He couldn't imagine anywhere else he'd rather be than here with Jilly, in her bed. They came together in a lover's quest, caressing, stroking, tasting. He hadn't thought he could become any more aroused, grow any harder. He wanted Jilly with a passion he'd never felt before.

Jilly's heart soared, and her body sang in Jeff's hands, making her feel virginal and cherished. Their eyes met as he hovered over her. His gaze revealed such longing, such hunger, that she felt like the most beautiful woman in the world.

"Now, Jeff. Love me now."

As he entered her, slowly, almost reverently, she arched to meet him. Her movement seemed to be the only encouragement he needed, and he thrust deeply in and out.

She closed her eyes, savoring the feel of him inside of her, trying hard to forget about tomorrow, about the future. Jeff was here with her now, and she had every intention of treasuring what she had this moment.

Her body responded to his, meeting each thrust until a blinding climax burst into a swirling rainbow of colors. She held on to each wave of pleasure, unwilling to let the moment end and intent on absorbing every bit of him.

As they lay in each other's arms, bodies glistening and the scent of their lovemaking in the air, they held tight, as though neither dared let go.

Would he pull away now? Find a reason to leave? The fear of sleeping alone nearly tore her in two.

Yet he didn't roll away. Didn't climb from bed.

Much to her surprise and pleasure he stayed all night long, holding her close, loving her again and again, each time more fulfilling than the last.

It seemed as though they'd joined forever, finding a pleasure and contentment they'd never found before.

But when dawn brought the light of day, Jilly felt him finally slip away.

As she promised, and even though it tore her apart, she feigned sleep and let the man she loved walk away, out of her bed, out of her house, out of her life.

# Chapter Thirteen

Jeff drove Jilly's car with no destination in mind. Just sitting behind the wheel helped to clear his thoughts.

The way he saw it, he had two options.

He could hightail it out of Rumor, or he could bite the bullet and marry his best friend, the woman he'd probably loved for years.

As weird as it might sound, marriage to Jilly wouldn't be so bad, not if he could manage to juggle his old life with being a husband and father. Would she agree to a long-distance arrangement? To having him fly back to Rumor one or two weekends a month?

Would it be enough for her?

The idea wasn't nearly as scary as it had once been—if she was willing. And he couldn't see any reason why she shouldn't agree to his conditions.

If anything, the community had accepted her and the baby so far. Marriage to him would solidify the respectability she'd always craved.

And if truth be known, he wouldn't be getting the short end of the stick. Marrying Jilly would have a definite upside. Last night had convinced him their sexual relationship was bound to be out of this world.

Making love to Jilly had been better than he could have imagined, and leaving her bed at dawn had been tough. Jeff had never been one to cuddle, but holding her while she slept had felt good and right.

She'd continued to sleep while he showered, and for a moment he'd thought of putting on a pot of coffee, maybe bringing her breakfast in bed.

But he hadn't. He needed time to think, time to sort out his thoughts, make a game plan he could live with.

And that's why he'd been driving around town aimlessly. He glanced at the clock on the dash— 10:45 a.m.

His stomach growled, alerting him to the fact he hadn't had supper last night.

Five minutes later he pulled into the parking lot of the Calico Diner. Maybe food would clear his head, help him think.

While he sat in the red vinyl booth, savoring a cup of coffee, he made up his mind. Now all he had to do was talk to Jilly, ask her if a compromise would work for her.

Jeff didn't think of himself as a romantic sort, but a drive out to Lake Monet might be the perfect place to talk about marriage and the future. A slow smile tugged at his lips. He'd have to ask the waitress to pack them a picnic lunch.

Wine was out of the question, but maybe he could pick up a bottle of sparkling apple cider at the general store. To help them celebrate.

Yep, a picnic at the lake would be perfect. Of course, a phone call to Jilly was definitely in order. He had slipped away in a quiet and pensive mood this morning, and even though he'd gotten things cleared up in his mind, she might be struggling with her own thoughts and worries.

After placing his order, Jeff picked up his cell phone and called Jilly's house.

She answered on the third ring. "Hello?"

"It's me."

She didn't respond right away, and he wondered if she was mad. Or hurt. Didn't she understand what a tough decision he'd had to make? Did she think it was easy to reassess his whole life's plan?

Finally, she asked, "Where did you run off to?"

"I had some thinking to do." He hoped that explanation would suffice. "Are you up for a picnic out at the lake?"

Again she paused. And for a moment he wondered whether she'd tell him to soak his head in a bucket of carnations. "I guess so."

"Will you be ready in fifteen minutes?"

"Sure."

He didn't detect any enthusiasm in her voice and wondered again whether she was angry. Well, as soon as she heard what he had to say, her mood would lift.

Or so he hoped.

Jilly and Jeff passed the apartments on State Street and headed toward Lake Monet. The Montana sky never looked as blue, the trees never so green and majestic.

"It's a pretty day," Jeff commented, then slid a glance across the seat. "Don't you think?"

"Yes, it is." Jilly couldn't help but wait for the sky to fall, for Jeff to tell her it was time to say goodbye. But she tried to keep her spirits up, tried to remain true to her word.

What she'd told him last night had come from the bottom of her heart; at least, the things she'd said out loud.

She'd fallen deeply in love with her best friend, yet she loved him enough not to cling to him. When it came time for Jeff to leave Rumor, she'd let him go with class and style, even though her heart would be torn in two.

Of course, she hadn't admitted to the secret of her heart and never would. Other than the lie of omission, everything she'd told him had been true.

What they'd shared last night hadn't been wrong.

And she wouldn't expect more than he was willing to give.

Their lovemaking had been beautiful and special. The sweet memory would last her a lifetime, since that's all she would be able to keep.

Hoping to put her best friend at ease, she leaned back in her seat and smiled. "I realize you'll be going back to Colorado soon. I hope you don't think I'll try to hold you here in Rumor." She shot a glance across the seat, saw him sitting rigidly behind the wheel.

"That's what I wanted to talk to you about," he said. "About me going back to Colorado, about me leaving you here."

Could Jilly read him like a book or what?

She continued to brush aside his pensive look, intending to make things easier for him. "Don't worry about getting on with your life, flyboy. Like I said, I'm not expecting anything you're not willing to give."

Jeff was willing to give a lot. His name. Financial support. And a long-distance marriage.

The marriage thing still left him gun-shy, of course. But he had to admit he would look forward to coming home for the best sex he'd ever had.

He turned down the drive that led to Lake Monet, one of several lakes in the Rumor area. No one remembered who had dubbed the pristine water, but legend had it that the colors that danced upon the surface reminded the townsfolk of a Monet painting.

"The water level is down," Jilly said, "and the

reflections are nowhere near as vivid as they were when we last picnicked. It's still pretty, though. Don't you think?"

It was, and he nodded. "You remember the last time we came here?"

She laughed. "Did you think I'd forgotten?"

He didn't suppose she had.

"You brought me out here to tell me you were leaving town."

Cripes. No wonder she'd seemed subdued when he suggested the picnic. She probably expected him to drop the bomb, to tell her he was taking off again.

In a way he supposed that was true. He was leaving. But he was also offering marriage, a small intimate wedding of course. Family only. And he'd be back in a few weeks, moving some of his stuff back to Rumor. Not all of it, but his good razor, the electric toothbrush, a few other personal items.

The bulk of his belongings would stay in the small studio apartment he'd continue to rent in Denver.

He glanced at the passing scenery, the towering pines, the wildflowers that dotted the hillside. "I've always found it easy to think out here."

"And to say goodbye."

"I didn't come out here to say goodbye," he said, but that wasn't entirely true. He'd never been able to snowball Jilly, and she knew something was up. But, heck, he couldn't just blurt it out.

He parked the car, grabbed the basket lunch he'd had the Calico Diner prepare, then walked alongside

Jilly as they made their way to the grassy area by the lake. The sun shone on their backs as they strode the pathway. A blue jay chattered from the treetops, and a light breeze kicked up the scents of pine and grass.

Had she purposely chosen to walk on the side of his bad arm?

If Jeff hadn't been wearing a cast, he'd have taken Jilly's hand in his or slipped an arm around her shoulder. It was a touchy-feely kind of day, yet he felt awkward and gangly, like a freshman at the senior prom.

Her floral scent mingled with the fresh air and pines, and he was struck with the urge to speak, to talk about what making love to her had done to him.

His tongue seemed to jam in his throat, and he wondered if he'd be able to find the words, to tell her the things a woman expected to hear at a time like this.

And what time was this?

He still wasn't entirely sure. Things with Jilly had never been stilted or awkward, yet here he was, struggling to find the right words.

They sat on the grass. Jilly kicked off her shoes and wiggled toes that bore pink nail polish. He'd never been as free and easy as she was, but for some reason, he wanted to shuck his inhibitions. Maybe it would help him say what needed to be said.

As they munched on fried chicken, potato salad

and slices of watermelon, Jeff managed to find his voice, as well as his courage.

"I'd like to marry you."

Jilly choked on a juicy chunk of melon.

"Are you okay?" Jeff wondered whether he should pat her on the back or just let her cough.

"I'm…all right." She coughed and sputtered again, then seemed to catch her breath.

Jeff's comment had taken Jilly aback. She couldn't possibly have heard him correctly. Everyone knew Jeff Forsythe wasn't the marrying kind. Needing some clarification, she asked, "What did you say?"

He seemed to hem and haw, as if he'd uttered something he hoped to retract. "I asked you to marry me."

That's what she thought he'd said, but he couldn't possibly mean it. Guilt and a sense of responsibility must have hit him terribly hard. She knew him too well. Marriage would tie him down, cramp his style. He'd said as much many times in the past.

"I have to admit, last night was terrific," she said. "Spectacular, even. But you certainly don't owe me a proposal because of it."

He kicked off his boots and removed his socks. She'd always thought he had interesting feet, and she fought the urge to play footsy, to run her toes along the top of his.

"I'm not suggesting the typical kind of marriage," he said.

She scrunched her nose. "What kind of marriage are you suggesting?"

"Something long-distance."

Married? In name only? And he thought she might actually consider something that bizarre? What was he thinking?

Pretending to act normal, to appear as though his suggestion made sense, she reached into the bag of chicken and pulled out a drumstick. "What do you mean by a long-distance marriage?"

He studied the lake, the sky and anything, it seemed, but her eyes. "Well, you know..."

She didn't know. In fact, she didn't have the foggiest notion what he meant. Had he fallen down and suffered a head injury? "I'm afraid I don't have a clue what you're talking about."

"We can get married, Jilly. And you can have a real wedding, if you want, with all the bells and whistles. But I'll keep my residence in Colorado."

And he thought this would appeal to her for *what* reason? What good was a husband who lived in another state? And for Pete's sake, Jeff never even thought to invite her to live with him in Colorado, not that she'd be excited about making a move like that, but at least he could suggest it.

She bit into the drumstick, even though her hunger had abated minutes before, and tried to chew on a tasteless mouthful of chicken.

The silence seemed to swallow them both into a

dark abyss. Finally she asked, "Why would we want to get married and live apart?"

"Well, it's one way to compromise. And it's a way to give the baby a name. My name."

If he'd flipped her off, she wouldn't have been more surprised. Weren't proposals supposed to have the words *I love you* interspersed somewhere?

She loved Jeff. And more than anything in the world, she wanted to hear him admit the same thing—with feeling, of course. And romantic fool that she was, she would even consider moving to Colorado and living in his two-room apartment.

But he didn't love her. Not in the right way. And his sympathy, pity and sacrifice on her behalf wasn't enough.

Pain gave way to anger. "My baby doesn't need your name."

"Okay," he said, "but marrying me might help you."

Help her? How noble of him to do his duty. He might have meant the offer to cheer her up, but his words had fallen flat.

Jilly's heart ached with disappointment. If Jeff loved her, she would give up her dreams in a heartbeat. She'd sell her shop and her home, move to Colorado and live in the studio apartment in which he kept his things but rarely stayed. "I don't need your help, Jeff. I'm doing just fine without you."

"But you'd do better as my wife."

Is that what he thought? That he was doing his

duty and making life better for her? She swallowed a rubbery piece of chicken and tossed what was left of the drumstick into the bag and stood. "Take me home."

"What's the matter?" he asked. "Don't you want to get married?"

"To you?" She placed her hands on her hips. "Absolutely not. You don't love me. Not in the right way. And quite frankly, I deserve more."

She marched back to the car, a million retorts brewing in her brain, none of them true.

"Jilly," he said, catching her swinging arm. "I didn't mean to upset you."

Oh no? She was furious.

No, scratch that. She was brokenhearted. But fury worked a lot better than tears. It seemed the best defense was truly a good offense. "Jeff, whatever it is we're tiptoeing on—friendship, relationship or whatever—is over. I want you to pack up your stuff and move on, whether it's Colorado or wherever you call home. Second best isn't good enough for me."

"Second best?"

"Whatever you're offering isn't enough. I want it all, a husband who loves me. And someday I'll find someone who won't think of me as some second-class citizen in need of a rescue."

"I don't think you're second class..."

"Oh, no?" Tears welled up in her eyes, but she fought them off with a burst of anger. "I wouldn't marry you if you were the last man on earth." She jerked away, presenting him with a view of her back as she walked to the car.

Jeff stood like a toad under a log and watched her stomp off. What was she wanting from him? Words of love and promises of forever?

He *did* love her. But he couldn't say what she apparently wanted to hear. The last person he'd admitted to loving was his mother.

The night of the gala at the country club, she'd come into his room, as pretty as a princess going to a ball.

He could still remember. Could still hear the last words they'd ever spoken. The promises they never kept.

*I wanted to tell you good-night, honey.*

*Can't I go, too, Mommy?*

*Not tonight. Helene will look after you. But tomorrow will be our special day. We'll have Henry take us on a drive down the coast, and we'll stop at that little shop that sells shaved ice. Won't that be fun?*

He'd nodded then, and she'd smiled.

If Jeff lived to be a hundred, he'd never forget the way her mouth quirked and her lively blue eyes glimmered with excitement. *And we'll stop at the amusement park at South Shore.*

*Can we ride the roller coaster, the great big one?*

*Of course.* She'd run her hand along his hair, as though making a memory. *You be good for Helene, and tomorrow we'll have an adventure by the shore. I love you, Jeff.*

*And I love you, too, Mommy. Have fun at the party.*

Helene had been the one who woke him up, told him his mother wouldn't ever come home again. He'd cried his eyes out before Aunt Carolyn arrived, her own eyes red and puffy, her own heart broken.

They'd grieved together, Carolyn for the sister she adored, and six-year-old Jeff for the mother who'd made up for his illegitimacy by loving him with all her heart and soul.

After the funeral Aunt Carolyn and Uncle Stratton had taken him home to the Kingsley ranch, promising to make him a part of the family. And they'd tried. Jeff couldn't fault them for that.

His aunt and uncle had wanted to adopt him, but he'd put up a fight. They'd also encouraged him to call them mom and dad. Again he'd refused by continuing to refer to them as Aunt Carolyn and Uncle Stratton.

He'd never been a real member of the Kingsley family, in a large part because he wouldn't allow it. For some reason, he'd always felt disloyal to his mother by becoming a Kingsley.

But maybe it was more than that. No one ever commented about his father, about the fact no one knew who the man was. It was a secret his mother had never shared. As Jeff grew older, he wondered if the Kingsleys' offer to adopt him had something to do with making him legitimate.

Maybe he was just plain stubborn. But he didn't want to be anyone other than Jeff Forsythe, a free spirit like his mother.

Sure, he loved his aunt and uncle—his cousins, too. And even though they never treated him as anything other than family, he'd never been able to utter the words that would make him a Kingsley.

*I love you* was too permanent, too binding. And saying it out loud, keeping the required promises of an admission like that would clip his wings for good.

He glanced at Jilly, saw her climb into the car and sit in the passenger seat and stoically face the front. She'd misunderstood his intentions, and he suspected that telling her he loved her, promising to stay in Rumor would make things better.

But he couldn't say the words, couldn't offer what she wanted.

Jilly sucked back the tears as Jeff drove her home. She'd lashed out at him in a desperate attempt to save face, to hold her head high.

Several times he tried to offer an apology of sorts, but as far as she was concerned, each attempt failed miserably.

"I never meant to imply you were anything other than special, Jilly. And I know that you can make it just fine without me. I'm sorry for hurting your feelings."

"No need to apologize," she said. How could he apologize for not loving her?

Never before had Jeff made her feel as though he felt sorry for her, as though she were still the little Davis waif who lived outside of town, a whoop and a holler from the strip joint.

She supposed his offer to marry her was made out of the kindness of his heart, but she needed more than a marriage in name only, needed more than his compassion.

"I'm not sure why you got so angry." He glanced across the seat.

She didn't suppose he would understand. An explanation might help, but how could she tell him her anger was actually disappointment, not to mention fear that she might cry in front of him, that she might reveal the secret of her heart?

"Don't worry about me. I'll be all right. I appreciate your offer to make things right, but I don't want your help." Not like that, anyway.

If things were different, if he loved her, she could compromise all she'd managed to build here in Rumor, all she'd ever hoped for. But there was one thing she wouldn't settle for.

Her marriage would be based on love. And love was a two-way street.

"Are we still friends?"

"Yes. We'll always be friends." She hoped the

words held true, but things had changed between them. She'd fallen head over heels for her best friend. And Jeff wasn't able to return her love.

She glanced out the window, studied the stately pine trees that grew along the side of the road.

Had making love to Jeff made things worse? Had it made his leaving more difficult to bear?

Or would the memory make things better, easier?

She swiped a tear from her eye.

It nearly tore Jeff up to see Jilly cry, to see her hurting and not be able to make things better. But what could he say or do to make things right, to backpedal and go back to the way they used to be?

"I'm sorry," he said. Sorry for not being able to say the words, for not being able to make the promises you need.

"Please don't be." She sniffled. "It's just hormones making me nuts. I'll be okay once you drop me off at home and I can take a nap."

He reached across the seat and took her hand, wishing he could do more, offer more. "I'm sorry for screwing things up between us and for hurting your feelings or stirring up your hormones. But I'm not sorry for making love to you, Jilly."

She turned to him and offered that chipped-tooth smile and squeezed his hand. "I'm glad you don't regret that. I don't, either."

He did, however, regret the damage their intimacy had wreaked upon their friendship, because he feared things would never be the same between them again.

"I didn't mean that things were over between us," Jilly said. "I was just angry and venting. I'd still like you to be Jaclyn's godfather."

"You bet."

But for some reason being the baby's godfather didn't seem to be enough. Nor did being Jilly's friend.

Still, Jeff couldn't say the words. Couldn't make the kind of commitment that she needed and deserved.

But he suspected it wasn't just because an *I love you* would be too binding.

Saying the words would also leave him vulnerable, like a little boy lying in bed, waiting for a trip to the seashore that never came.

## Chapter Fourteen

After dropping Jilly off at her house and promising to bring her car back later in the afternoon, Jeff drove twelve miles down Kingsley Avenue until he reached the sprawling ranch on the outskirts of Rumor.

The vast estate had never felt completely like home, so, he wasn't sure why he felt compelled to go to the place where he'd grown up. He supposed it was because he'd spent too much time driving aimlessly through Rumor. Going home to the ranch seemed like the right thing to do.

He turned onto the tree-lined entrance and drove through the massive iron gates that impressed some people and intimidated others. When he reached the house, he parked near one of the many rose gardens his aunt had planted throughout the parklike grounds, climbed from the car and strode toward the house.

At the top of the steps he reached the front door

and paused by the bell. The last two times he'd come to the Kingsley ranch, his cousin Maura had met him in the yard, welcomed him with a hug and led him into the house. But this time no one was in sight.

It had been so long since he'd lived here that he contemplated ringing to announce his arrival, then waiting like a guest. But Aunt Carolyn would probably shoot him if she answered the door and found him standing on the porch like a visitor passing through town.

Instead, he rang the bell, then let himself in. It seemed like a reasonable compromise.

"It's me," he called from the marble-tiled foyer.

Before he could reach the living room, Aunt Carolyn swept into sight.

"Jeff! What a lovely surprise." She gave him a hug that he actually welcomed. Her imported, spice-scented perfume enveloped him and triggered warm memories of his earlier years. "I'm so glad you stopped by."

He wasn't sure what he was doing here, what excuse to offer. Maybe he just wanted to touch base with his Kingsley roots. Or perhaps it was to feel close to his mother. Seeing Aunt Carolyn had always brought on thoughts of his mom—although usually her loss and absence. But his aunt also seemed to provide a touchstone for him.

Carolyn placed a soft, manicured hand upon his cheek, and he felt the urge to hold it there, to keep it close and savor the maternal expression.

"What's the matter?" she asked.

"Nothing. I thought I'd stop by to say hello. That's all."

Yet there seemed to be another reason he couldn't quite put his finger on. To get some advice, some guidance maybe? He wasn't sure, but it felt natural to be here. And comforting.

"It's so nice to have you home, even for a short visit. Why don't you come out onto the patio? I've just poured myself an iced tea, and you can join me."

He followed her to the kitchen, where she prepared a new glass and added a sprig of mint. In all his travels, tea had never tasted the same. His aunt prepared a refreshing, mint-laced concoction that defied explanation but hit the spot.

They sat outside at one of the patio tables, on cushioned wrought-iron chairs.

"Where's Jilly?" Carolyn asked.

"Home." He glanced at the glass tabletop, then scanned the lush gardens where he and Maura used to play hide-and-seek, sometimes to the exasperation of Pete, the head gardener.

Aunt Carolyn watched him over the rim of her glass, seeing, he suspected, far more than he'd become adept at hiding. Of course, she'd always had that knack, always knew what her cubs had been up to whenever they'd left the den.

"Something is bothering you, Jeff."

He wasn't used to confiding in his aunt, although he wasn't sure why. She'd always been good to him and made no bones about loving him as one of her sons. Maybe that's why he'd come today, to bounce his thoughts off her. "I asked Jilly to marry me."

"That's wonderful, dear." His aunt beamed as though he'd told her he won the lottery or had been invited for tea at the White House. "Have you set a date?"

Jeff shook his head and blew out an exasperated sigh. "Jilly said no—among other things."

His aunt studied the condensation on her glass, then drew a line in the moisture with a pink-polished nail. "Did she give you a reason why?"

"Not exactly." He raked a hand through his short hair. He was still trying to understand what had gone wrong. "For some reason she thought I was trying to do her a favor."

"Is that what you were trying to do?"

He supposed he was, to an extent. But it went further than that, deeper. Yet it was hard to voice his worries, his fears. His feelings. "I can't give Jilly what she wants."

"And what's that?"

"I'm not even sure anymore."

They sat quietly for a while, Jeff struggling with his thoughts and Aunt Carolyn allowing him the time to do so. In recent years she'd seemed to finally understand him, to respect his need to keep a distance, to make his own decisions, to follow his own path in life.

"I suggested a long-distance marriage," Jeff said. "I think Jilly wants a full-time husband."

"I see."

Jeff didn't know what she saw. He sure as hell didn't have a clear picture. His best friend had turned him inside out, and he wasn't sure about anything anymore. He wished Aunt Carolyn would give him a clue, since he was still trying to sort things out himself. It was all so confusing and complicated.

"Do you love her?" his aunt asked.

"Huh?"

A glimmer shone in Carolyn's eye, and she smiled. "Do you love Jilly?"

Yeah. He loved her, but that wasn't the point. Or was it? "I can't say what she wants to hear."

"If you can't say you love her, is it because you don't?" Aunt Carolyn eyed him sagely, as though she knew exactly what was on his mind.

And, no doubt she did. His aunt had probably waited years to hear him say those very words to her, too.

"I do love Jilly. In fact, I probably have for years, but recently things have changed. They've gotten more complex."

Aunt Carolyn reached across the table and took his hand. "Has your friendship deepened?"

She could say that again. Making love to Jilly had really changed things. And the fact was, once would never be enough. Sex with anyone else had lost its appeal.

Jilly had certainly clipped his wings on a sexual level. Emotional, too, he supposed. "Our friendship has become more intense, to say the least. Of course, she got mad at me earlier today and told me she wouldn't marry me if I was the last man on earth."

A soft smile tugged at his aunt's lips, as though she could decipher a woman's words, which was probably true.

Jeff had always been able to read Jilly before, when they were just friends, but not anymore. Things were different now. Maybe it was the hormones that had complicated things between them.

But instead of the pregnancy hormones, he feared that whatever chemicals controlled his heart were to blame.

"Your mother was a unique and intricate woman, much like you are, Jeff. But she always knew her own mind."

He shot his aunt a puzzled look. "Are you saying I don't know my own mind?"

"You always have, but in this case I think your heart is in the way." She reached a hand across the table, the sunlight causing her impressive diamond wedding ring to glisten like magic. "I've always known that you've loved us, Jeff, but you've never said the words. For some reason you've always held that part of yourself back."

What she said had been true, and he suspected that's why she'd taken him to see that shrink in Billings when he was a kid. But the doctor hadn't been able to get Jeff to crack, to be anything other than who he was.

Jeff remembered the play therapy sessions, where he refused to participate in any of the stupid games the doctor had suggested.

He pushed the wrought-iron chair away from the table and stood. Sitting down made him feel fenced in, vulnerable. He walked along the patio, gazed out onto the grassy slope, the roses blooming in the garden.

"If you love Jilly," his aunt said softly to his back, "and if she loves you, there ought to be a way to compromise, a way for both of you to have what you want and need."

Jeff nodded, but he didn't speak. He didn't trust himself to open his mouth. What had Jilly said to him?

*You don't love me. Not in the right way. And quite frankly, I deserve more.*

He did love her, and he damn sure loved her in the right way. But he couldn't say it, couldn't make the required commitment that would follow a profession like that.

And she was right; she did deserve more than he'd offered.

He walked the length of the patio, then turned and walked it again, pacing like a caged mountain lion. He thought of Jilly's smile, of her laughter and the night they'd given in to temptation, to passion, coming together in a joining so sweet that he wasn't likely to ever experience it again—unless it was with Jilly.

That ever-present ache grew deep in his heart, becoming more and more difficult to ignore, to hide.

His thoughts drifted to the baby that grew inside her, a little girl who sucked her thumb and had already become inexplicably real to Jeff. For some crazy reason he felt committed to the baby, bonded to a child he'd yet to meet.

"Your mother was effervescent and had a wild side," Aunt Caroline said, "but she was good-hearted. Had your father been the right man, she would have settled down and blossomed into a beautiful, loving wife and mother. And she might be alive today."

Several times Jeff had quizzed his mother about his dad, but she'd never gone into much detail. After she died, and he went to live with the Kingsleys, he'd questioned his aunt. She'd remained tight-lipped about his father, only to say she hadn't met the man.

"Tell me what you know about my dad," Jeff said. It wasn't a question coming from a kid, but a man needing to know.

"Your mother wouldn't tell me anything about him, other than the fact that he was married. Apparently, he'd kept that secret from her, too, until after she told him she was pregnant."

"Do you know his name?"

"No. But your mother refused to let her own marital status get in the way of her love for you. She held her head high in spite of the whispers, and when you were born, there wasn't a mother in the world who'd been prouder, happier or more loving. You meant the world to her."

It was true, and Jeff knew it.

As much as he'd cared for his aunt, as much as she'd tried to get him to talk to her, to share his grief and his feelings about his mom, he'd never been able to do so…before today.

He studied the woman who'd raised him, the woman who'd offered her heart and her home. It was time to level with her, he supposed. "My mom's last words to me were 'I love you.'"

"That doesn't surprise me a bit, Jeff. You were the light of her life. She loved you dearly."

"I told her I loved her, too. And then she left." And never came back.

"Perhaps that's why you find it difficult to admit your love to others."

"Maybe so."

Jeff loved Jilly. And he did want to marry her. But was saying the words out loud the only thing that worried him? What about making the kind of commitment she needed? Could he give up flying? The excitement of being on call, taking off at a moment's notice?

He didn't know. Either way, he felt as though a veil had been lifted, his thoughts and feelings sorted.

"Thanks for talking to me, Aunt Carolyn." He

bent down and gave her a hug. "I just needed to get some things straight in my mind."

"I'm glad I could help." His aunt stood and walked with him toward the sliding door that led to the front of the house. "I love you, Jeff."

He paused and took her hand. "Yeah, I know." Then he gave her a smile. "I...do, too."

"I know." She brushed a kiss upon his cheek. "But you'll find the more you admit to loving, the easier it gets."

Would it get easier? He hoped so.

As he headed Jilly's car home, back to her little house on Lost Lane, he agonized over his words, over his decision.

But one thing remained true. He loved Jilly Davis with his whole heart. And somehow, someway, he had to find the courage to open his heart and soul, to tell her.

To ask her to marry him—again.

Maybe this time, if he got the words right, she'd say yes.

Jilly was waiting in the backyard for Posey to do her doggy business when she heard a car pull into the drive.

*Her* car.

Jeff was back.

Her heart ached, but she knew it was time. Time to tell him goodbye and let him return to Colorado, where he belonged. She waited for Posey before going back inside, mostly because she would have someone to provide some comfort when Jeff left her life for good.

Most women would be angry that he'd slipped out quietly after a night of lovemaking, but Jilly had expected it. So how could she be mad?

Sure, she was hurt. But she'd known it was coming and had understood the consequences. Still, that didn't keep her heart from aching, her mind from dreaming of things that would never be.

When Posey dashed up to the back porch, Jilly went in with her and followed the dog into the living room, where Jeff now stood, more handsome than ever. She felt like a lone bowling pin, standing front and center, waiting for the last ball of the game to be thrown, but she managed to conjure a smile.

"Hey," he said. "Let's go for a ride."

Out to the lake again? No, thanks. If he had any goodbyes to say, he could get it over with right here. She crossed her arms and leaned her weight on one foot. "I'm not up for a ride. It's Sunday, and I have things to do before work tomorrow."

"But it'll just take a few minutes."

Actually, she'd done everything that had to be done while he'd been gone, but he didn't need to know that. "I don't want any fancy speeches, Jeff. If it's time for you to go, then let's just say goodbye here."

His expression grew serious, as though her words

took him aback. But she knew where this was going, and so did he.

"I hadn't planned to take you out to the lake," he said.

"No? Then where did you want to go?"

"To MonMart."

The man was full of surprises. Why did he want her to go with him to the town superstore? She glanced over her shoulder, toward the spare rooms that were bursting with baby items and toys. "What do you want to buy?"

"More stuff for the baby."

Jilly shook her head. "You're crazy. I need a bigger house before I can possibly fit anything else in either of those rooms."

"Humor me," he said. Then he took her hand and led her outside and into the car.

Minutes later they entered a bustling MonMart. It seemed everyone in town had decided to go shopping on Sunday afternoon.

Jeff held her hand, and she relished the strength of his grip, the warmth of his touch. It might be years before she ever touched him like this again, which sent a lingering jolt of sadness to her soul and left a gaping hole in her heart.

They walked the aisles of Russell Kingsley's megastore, dodging carts, passing one shopper after another. Mrs. Evans, the church organist, waved to them from a table near the bakery, where she shared a sweet roll and a cup of coffee with two other gray-haired ladies.

It was no wonder that people with time on their hands found shopping a pleasant diversion, and at times a social event. Besides, MonMart not only offered a ton of discounted merchandise, it also provided the townspeople with an enormous parking lot to hold various community events.

Jilly smiled and waved in greeting but continued to follow Jeff through the throng of shoppers. Instead of heading toward the toys or the baby department, he led her to a purple-and-red-lighted service desk in the middle of the store, where a microphone had been set up to announce hourly specials.

"What are you looking for?" she asked, assuming he was trying to find a clerk to ask for directions. People got lost in this store all the time. Children, enamored by the bright lights and colorful displays, wandered from their mothers, harried housewives who searched the many aisles for the advertised bargains.

But the lost-and-found announcements were not merely made for children. More often than not, a husband went to automotive and ended up in garden, only to lose his wife somewhere between the housewares and the produce department.

Not seeing a clerk nearby, Jilly scanned the aisles nearest her, hoping to spot someone who could answer Jeff's question.

When he dropped her hand and reached for the microphone, she thought he'd surely lost his mind.

"What are you doing?"

He merely smiled, then lifted the mike to his mouth and pushed the button that would allow him to broadcast throughout the store.

"May I have your attention?" he asked.

"Put that thing down," she said in an exasperated whisper. "Are you crazy?"

"Yes, Jilly, I am." His voice boomed throughout the store. "I'm crazy about you."

Her heart thudded in her chest. He'd lost it. Being grounded in Rumor had done something to his mind, his sensibilities. Grabbing a microphone in a store and pulling a silly stunt like this was more Jilly's style. Not Jeff's.

"I have something to tell you, honey, and I don't care who hears."

Oh, Lordy. Jilly looked to her right and to her left. Did MonMart have bouncers? Someone who hauled troublemaking shoppers out of the store?

"This is Jeff Forsythe," he said, "just in case any of you are wondering. And this isn't an announcement of a flashing-light bargain. It's just a man baring his heart and soul to a very special lady."

A flood of heat swept across Jilly's cheeks, as embarrassment washed over her. The horde of once-busy shoppers pulled their carts to a halt and watched, listening to hear what Jeff had to say.

She reached for the mike, but he pulled it back and grinned.

"Put that down," she mouthed. "Before the men in white coats haul you away."

"Jilly Davis, I want to marry you." His eyes pierced hers, drawing them into their sky-blue depths, but she wasn't about to fall prey.

She'd already let him know what she thought about the idea of a long-distance marriage and him offering her and the baby his name just so they could save face in the community. Crossing her arms, she shook her head. "No."

"I want to be your husband and live in Rumor. And I don't care what I have to give up to make it happen. You're worth it, Jilly."

Live in Rumor? Give up his freedom, his come-and-go-as-you-please life? No way could she let him do that. She swiped at a tear that slipped down her cheek. "I never asked you to stay in town nor will I allow it."

"Jilly, you're my very best friend," Jeff announced, "and I want to let everyone in the community know that you're also the best thing that ever happened to me."

It wasn't quite what she wanted, although he was getting awfully darn close. She couldn't let him do it, couldn't let him sacrifice his happiness for hers. She loved him too much. "Marriage is built on more than friendship, Jeff. Now, put down that microphone and let's get out of here."

"I haven't said this to anyone in eighteen years, honey, but I'm saying it now." He paused, as if his jaw had grown rusty and he needed to work out the kinks. "I love you more than anything in this world, Jilly Davis. And I don't want to live my life without you. Will you marry me?"

Her heart swelled to the bursting point, and tears blurred her vision. That stubborn, crazy pilot who turned her heart inside out, had just proposed in the weirdest, yet the sweetest and most touching, way possible.

Jilly threw herself into his arms—one good and the other still sporting a cast—and pressed her mouth to his.

The mike dropped to the floor, the speaker screeched in an ear-shattering protest, and the entire store erupted in applause and cheers.

When they came up for air and the kiss ended, Jilly said, "I love you, flyboy, more than anything in the whole wide world. And I won't ask you to give up anything. We'll work this out. Somehow."

He sent her a smile that touched her soul, and eyes the color of the Montana sky glimmered with love. "Then let's go home, Jilly. I want to seal my proposal with more than a kiss."

Jeff could scarcely believe how good it felt to tell Jilly—and all of MonMart—that he loved her. He'd been holding in his feelings for so damn long it felt as though he'd been set free.

And maybe he had.

As they walked out of the store, Jilly squeezed his hand. "As long as you love me, I'll figure out how to make a long-distance marriage work." She looked up at him with so much love, so much devotion, that his heart swelled.

It was as though a dam had broken, releasing a torrent of feelings he'd never known he had.

"Hell, Jilly, now that you've got me thinking all kinds of sappy things, I'm not sure I want to be in Colorado when I've got you and the baby waiting for me here."

Jilly laughed. "Let's not talk about Colorado now. Can you drive a bit faster? I'd like to get you home and show you how good being married to me is going to be."

"Now you're talking."

Ten minutes later they arrived at the little house on Lost Lane.

*Home.*

Jeff would live here now, with a wife he adored and a soon-to-be-born daughter. As he scanned the front yard, the carpet of grass, the maple tree, the marigolds that lined the walk, the red geraniums in a wooden tub near the porch, his first chore as a husband and daddy came to mind.

"I'm going to the hardware store on Monday," he said. "And after picking up the supplies, I'm going to build you that picket fence you've always wanted. It shouldn't be too hard, do you think?"

Jilly turned and gave him a hug. "With a broken arm? That might be a bit tricky. Why don't you wait until the cast comes off?"

"Maybe you're right, but I'm still going to measure the yard and purchase the supplies. When I get this fool thing off my arm, the fence will be my first undertaking."

"What's gotten into you, Jeff? Where's the guy I used to know?"

"Love's gotten into me." He cupped her cheek and brushed a kiss across her mouth. "And if I didn't have a bum arm, I'd carry you over the threshold."

She looked up at him, blessing him with a smile that promised love and forever. "By the time your arm heals, I'll be too big to carry."

He broke into a grin. "Don't count on it. I'm strong enough to carry my wife and my baby."

His wife and his baby. For a guy who'd skirted home and hearth for years, Jeff was sure looking forward to having a family, a wife and child of his own.

As they entered the living room, Posey yapped in greeting, then flew across the floor and skidded into their feet.

Correction, Jeff thought, picking up the dog. He had a home, a wife, a baby *and a dog*. "Better get used to me, Dust Mop. I'm part of the family now."

The goofy little pooch licked his cheek in welcome and approval.

"I'll fix Posey something to eat and put her on the back porch," Jilly said.

"Good idea. I plan to keep you occupied for the rest of the afternoon and evening, and you're the only one I want to hear whimper."

"How do you propose to do that?" she asked, a naughty glimmer in her eyes.

He kissed her cheek. "Just feed the dog, and I'll meet you in the bedroom."

That afternoon, with the window open and a soft breeze blowing through the frilly, white cotton curtains in Jilly's room, Jeff showed her with his heart and his body just how much he loved her.

And she showed him right back, matching each thrust, each climax, each lingering caress.

As the sun sank into the western Montana sky, Jeff traced the gentle curve of Jilly's hip. "We've got a wedding to plan. How does next Saturday afternoon sound to you?"

"What kind of wedding are you talking about? I'd like something simple and small."

"Okay. I'll talk to Pastor Rayburn tomorrow and see if he can marry us. I'd like to keep it small, too. Just family and a few friends."

"I'd like to invite Emmy," she said. "And maybe Ash, if that's all right with you."

Jeff brushed a strand of hair from her cheek. "I don't see any reason why not. Ash was always good to you."

Jilly's eyes glimmered like melted chocolate. "I love you, flyboy."

"I love, you, too," he said, the words coming out easier the second time around. It felt good to express the feeling bubbling up inside. And it felt damn good to hold Jilly close.

As the light of day slipped away for the night, they basked in the love they found in each other and considered the future that lay before them.

Jeff had some calls to make and a trip or two to Colorado. But he would stay in Rumor full-time, to be Jilly's husband and her baby's father.

No matter what he had to give up.

# Chapter Fifteen

Jeff made most of the wedding arrangements so Jilly could finish the work that had backed up while she'd taken time away from the florist shop. Of course, yesterday afternoon, when Maura took Jilly into Billings to purchase a wedding dress, Jeff stayed behind to man Jilly's Lilies.

He answered the phone and took orders, one of which was from Bud Hendrickson, a cross-country truck driver who spent more time at Joe's Bar when he was in town than at home with his wife and children.

Now, at the worktable, surrounded by flowers and floral scents, Jilly labored on Bud's arrangement of light-yellow roses and calla lilies. She cut a strip of white satin ribbon and began to weave a bow.

Bud had ordered the flowers for his mother-in-law, Harriet Barksdale, a widow who was president of the Ladies' Aid Society at the Rumor Community Church.

Jilly suspected the floral arrangement was meant to be a peace offering. She hadn't read the card he'd carefully written and sealed in an envelope, but she concluded it was an apology of sorts.

Of course, all she had to go by was the word of local gossips, which didn't mean that it was entirely true. Some of the tales became grossly exaggerated as each link of the rumor mill embellished a portion. But this time Jilly figured the bulk of the story was legit.

Bud, it seemed, had made a big mistake when he played a practical joke on his wife's widowed, straitlaced mother. His humor, according to several gossip-prone sources, had fallen flat.

After an alleged, rip-roaring night at Joe's Bar, Bud replaced the widow's front porch light with a red bulb that he'd found somewhere, a prank the prim-and-proper woman didn't appreciate, especially since she'd set her sights on Pastor Rayburn, the distinguished—and single—minister of the Rumor Community Church.

Jilly wondered if the widow would forgive her wayward son-in-law when she read the card and saw the flowers.

Maybe not.

Since Bud tended to be a regular at Joe's Bar, Jilly suspected his drinking and carousing might not be as easy to forgive, and the prank had merely been the last piece of straw on an already teetering pile.

She adjusted the bow and studied the finished product. Not bad. As she cleared away the stems and leaves from the table, she thought about the floral arrangements and bouquets she'd prepare tomorrow.

In the past she'd prepared the flowers for other people's weddings, but this time she would make her own. She looked forward to creating two bouquets, three corsages, five boutonnieres and several sprays to grace the altar. A bit of herself—her hopes and dreams—would go into each blossom, each ribbon and bow.

Two more days until the ceremony.

She could hardly wait.

It would be a small wedding, with only Maura and Russell standing up with the bride and groom. Jilly's only disappointment was that Emmy couldn't be her maid of honor.

She'd called Emmy on Sunday evening, and the two friends talked on the phone for nearly two hours, chatting about the life changes they'd each experienced in the past few years, the hopes they had and the plans they'd made.

Emmy had a medical seminar in Billings this coming weekend, and there was no way she could get out of it, especially at this late date. Jilly certainly understood, but she wasn't about to postpone her wedding any longer than necessary. She couldn't wait to be Jeff's wife. Saturday still seemed to be a long way off.

By the time she and Emmy had run out of words to say, they'd agreed to meet for dinner in Big Timber, two weeks from next Tuesday.

Yes, life was coming together for Jilly.

The bell chimed on the front door, and she glanced up from her work, hoping to see Jeff.

Instead, Ash McDonough stood before her.

She offered him a smile. "Hey, what's up?"

He removed his hat, revealing dark-brown hair. "I came by to congratulate you on your marriage."

"Thank you."

He glanced at the hat in his hands, then gazed at her with gray eyes that couldn't hide the burdens he carried. "I'd like to attend the wedding, Jilly, but I think it's best that I stay away. The town isn't ready to turn the other cheek yet. And I don't want to do anything to make your day less than perfect."

She wanted to argue with him, but she'd seen the reaction of people at her shower. Their disapproval had probably hurt him more than he was willing to admit. She supposed he wasn't up to a repeat of the cool reception he'd received. "I'll miss not having you there, Ash. I've always counted you as a special friend."

"I appreciate that." He studied her for a moment, then cast her a familiar grin. "You've got a happy glow I've never seen before, Jilly. Being in love sits well with you."

She broke into a smile that had dogged her all week. "I'm happy, Ash. Really happy, for the first time in my life. Sometimes I want to pinch myself, but if it is a dream, I don't want to wake up."

"You deserve to have it all. And I hope the future brings you more of the same."

"Thanks." Jilly's heart went out to the solemn man who stood before her. "You deserve some happiness, too."

"Yeah, well that may come with time." He shrugged, disregarding her concern. "I'd better head back to the ranch."

"My advice still stands," Jilly said. "You need to give Emmy a call."

Ash nodded, then slipped on his hat and walked out the door.

Jilly sympathized, but Ash was right. It would take time for the folks in Rumor to forgive and forget.

She went back to work, plucking a stray calla lily from the base and rearranging it to suit her artistic need for perfection.

The bell on the door rang again, and this time her glance was rewarded with a glimpse of Jeff. He grinned from ear to ear, and excitement burned bright in his eyes.

She ignored the rebellious lily and went to his arms. "You're in a chipper mood."

"The best," he said, giving her a lingering hug. "Guess what I've been up to."

"What?" She pulled away so that she could search his face for a clue. "Planning our wedding?"

"Besides that." His silly grin suggested he'd been doing something other than inviting people to the church and speaking to the minister and organist.

She gave him a playful sock on the arm. "Okay, spill it. What's going on?"

"I resigned my job with the forestry service."

"And?" she said, knowing he was independently wealthy but too active to become permanently retired.

"I talked to Dev Holmes and offered my services to the new business he's starting."

"What kind of business is that?" She knew Jeff and Dev had known each other for years, meeting first out at the airfield. Did the business have something to do with planes? She couldn't imagine another occupation putting a smile on Jeff's face like that.

"It's an outfitting service based in Rumor. We'll be flying sportsmen looking for remote hunting and fishing spots." He grabbed her hand and gave it a squeeze, his eyes searching hers. "What do you think, Jilly?"

"I think that's wonderful." But would it make him happy? And what about MAFFS? Jeff had been trained to fight forest fires. Would he give all that up?

Her thoughts turned to the fire that continued to blaze outside of Rumor, the fire he'd been sent to fight before he'd become injured. "Are you sure that's what you want to do?"

"I talked to my commander. He's going to call me in whenever there's a major fire. Can you handle me being away for emergencies like that?"

She wrapped her arms around his neck. "Of course I can. I just couldn't handle you being stationed in Colorado and coming home a couple times a month."

"I'm glad we found a compromise, something that would make us both happy." Jeff brushed a kiss across her lips.

All of a sudden Jilly gasped and pulled away.

"What's the matter?" His eyes grew wide, fearful.

"The baby," she said, reaching for the flutter that seemed to tumble in her tummy. "She moved. I've been feeling these little twinges before, but this one was much stronger."

Jeff reached a hand to her womb and stood there for the longest time, but the baby didn't move again. And Jilly wasn't sure if he could have felt it, anyway. The movement was so faint, so tiny, so precious, she scarcely felt it herself.

But she had. Her daughter was real and growing bigger every day. Soon she would be big enough to live in the real world.

"Jaclyn will move again," Jilly said, liking the way the baby's name lingered on her breath, her heart. "As she gets bigger, I'm sure you'll be able to feel her movements. I've heard some of the kicks in the last month can be pretty strong."

Jeff bent on one knee and placed his face against Jilly's tummy. "Listen up, little girl. This is your daddy, so you might as well get used to my voice. Mommy and I are going to take good care of you, so be ready for lots of love when you've grown big enough to join our family."

Then he looked up at Jilly and smiled, his love as bright and vivid as the flowers that surrounded them.

"I can't wait until Saturday," Jilly said.

"Neither can I. I want the rest of our lives to begin." Then Jeff sealed his words with a long, loving kiss.

The day of the wedding had finally arrived. The wind conveniently shifted, lifting the smoky haze the fire often cast upon the town.

The air was clean and mountain fresh, with little hint of the ash and smoke that sometimes lingered. The summer sun rose high in the Montana sky, burning warm and bright and casting a magical glow through the stained-glass windows of the church.

In the small choir room off the sanctuary, Jeff stood before a mirror, trying to straighten a cummerbund and tie with nervous fingers.

Uncle Stratton and Jeff's cousins—Russell, Reed and Tag—watched his clumsy struggle.

"Need some help?" his uncle asked.

"Sure." Jeff turned from the mirror and let his uncle step in.

It seemed a normal response. Time and again, the man had stepped up to the plate, teaching Jeff to ride a bike, pointing out an easier way to figure out an algebraic equation.

Stratton tugged at the cummerbund, then adjusted the pesky tie.

Jeff had always appreciated his uncle's efforts to help, but never told him to his face. No time like the present, he supposed.

He caught the gray-haired man's eye. "You've always been there for me, and I want you to know how much that means to me."

Stratton placed a hand on Jeff's shoulder. "I was glad to do it, son."

*Son.*

That said it all.

Stratton had treated Jeff like a son from the first day he crossed the threshold of the Kingsley ranch, scolding him when he needed it, instructing him how to behave in social settings, convincing Aunt Carolyn to agree to flying lessons on his sixteenth birthday. And probably most important of all, teaching him to be a man.

"A long time ago," Jeff said, "Aunt Carolyn told me I could call you two Mom and Dad. I wasn't ready to then. But if the offer still stands—"

Stratton embraced him and patted his back. "I'd be proud to be your father, son."

Jeff wasn't sure where all the moisture came from, but his eyes grew watery. "I…uh, love you…Dad."

It felt good, right, especially today, as the foundation of the future was laid.

Tears spilled onto Jeff's cheeks. The emotional response embarrassed him, but only until he looked up and caught the glistening eyes of his cousins.

*His brothers.*

For once in his life, the mushy stuff didn't bother him at all.

They were family.

*Kingsleys.*

And Jeff was *not* just a shirttail relative. He was one of them. He glanced first at Russell, the oldest, then Tag and Reed, the once-towering role models he'd looked up to while growing up. "I want to thank you guys for taking me under your wings, for accepting me like your little brother."

"We were happy to do it, Jeff, even though you were a pain at times." Russell slid him a crooked grin and placed a hand on his shoulder. "Besides, having you around gave us someone to pick on, especially since we caught hell whenever we teased Maura."

Before Jeff could comment further, a knock sounded at the door. Aunt Carolyn's voice asked, "Is it all right if I come in?"

"Sure."

As stately and elegant as any first lady or monarch, Carolyn entered the small room with grace and charm. The auburn-haired woman was still as pretty as Jeff remembered, her blue eyes just as bright.

"Why, look at you," Carolyn said, scanning the room and admiring the tuxedoed men she loved. "I've never seen a more handsome group."

"Listen," Jeff said to the woman who had raised him as her own, "while I'm in a sappy mood, I want to tell you something."

"What's that?" she asked.

"I love you, Aunt Carolyn."

There, he said it. And he meant it, too.

Tears welled in her eyes, and she drew him into a warm embrace. "I knew you've always felt that way, but it's so nice to hear the words. I love you, too, Jeff."

"And if it's all right," Jeff continued, saying what had needed to be said years ago, "I'm going to start referring to you and Uncle Stratton as my parents."

"It's more than all right," Aunt Carolyn said. "It's what I've always hoped and prayed for."

"I hate to put the damper on this weepy mood," Reed said, "but it's time for the wedding to start. And I've got to get back to the fire command post."

"I'll check on the girls," Carolyn said. Then she looked at Jeff. "Are you ready?"

"You bet." Jeff flashed his aunt a smile. "Thanks… Mom."

Carolyn nodded, then reached into the small purse that matched her pale-lavender suit and withdrew a lacy handkerchief. She blotted her eyes, before stepping outside and softly closing the door.

Jilly stood in a small, walnut-paneled room off the back side of the church, with Maura at her side.

She peered into the floor-length mirror that graced the oak door and studied her reflection. The ivory-colored gown she and Maura had chosen was in the Renaissance style, with an empire waist that allowed room for her tummy, which seemed to be expanding every day.

"I'm so nervous," Jilly confessed.

"Don't be," her soon-to-be cousin-in-law said. "You look beautiful."

"Thanks."

Maura, too, looked pretty in the soft-green gown she wore. With red hair like her mother's, the petite young woman had grown to be a beauty.

"I've never seen Jeff so happy," Maura said. "I think you and he are the only ones who didn't expect the two of you to fall in love. We've all been speculating for years."

Jilly flashed her a smile. "Well, the speculating is over. I love your cousin with all of my heart."

"And he loves you." Maura returned her smile. "You two have your whole lives ahead of you."

That they did.

Jilly took a deep breath and blew out a sigh. "You

know, when Jeff and I decided to get married, I didn't want to wait until Saturday. But we needed time to put together a little wedding."

"I wish we could have had more time to plan, but everything is going to be perfect."

A knock sounded, and when Maura opened the door, Carolyn stepped inside, eyes glimmering with tears. "You look lovely, Jilly."

"Thank you."

She kissed Jilly, then Maura. "Are you girls ready?"

As ready as they'd ever be, Jilly supposed. "Is it time?"

"Yes." Carolyn picked up the simple yet elegant bouquet of tulips Jilly would carry and handed them to her. "Is it all right if Stratton comes in?"

Jeff's uncle would walk Jilly down the aisle. And although she'd always been a bit intimidated by him while growing up, the man had been warm, friendly and accepting of her. "Of course. Let him come in."

When Carolyn opened the door, a tuxedoed Stratton entered the women's domain. He cast a glance at Jilly and his daughter. A grin crossed his face, and his eyes lit up. "You both look stunning." Then he lifted his arm for Jilly to take. "Let's not keep Jeff waiting."

Carolyn exited the small room first and alerted Pastor Rayburn that the services were about to begin. Then she nodded to Mrs. Evans, who sat at the organ.

Within moments, music filled the quaint little church that was nearly bursting with guests, even though Jilly and Jeff had planned to keep things simple and small.

The Kingsleys, it seemed, had a ton of close friends and relatives, none of whom could be excluded. Even with the late notice, very few passed up the invitation to wish Jeff and Jilly well.

Up front, at the altar, Jeff and Russell stood solemnly waiting for the ceremony to begin.

The processional began uniquely, with Tag escorting his mother down the aisle to her seat, then joining his wife, Linda, in the same pew.

Pretty little Samantha, Tag's daughter, scattered rose petals on the white walkway and smiled happily, pleased to be part of the wedding.

Reed escorted Maura down the aisle, and as she reached the front of the church, he slipped into the first pew, next to Susannah, Russell's wife, who held baby Mei, a smiling, dark-haired cherub who'd recently joined the family.

Stratton stooped to whisper in Jilly's ear before the wedding march began. "Jeff is our son, as far as I'm concerned. And Jilly, if you're willing, I'd like to consider you my daughter. My wife feels the same way."

Tears, seeming to be ever present this past week, flooded Jilly's eyes, and she struggled to whisper the words that filled her heart. "Thank you, Stratton. Your acceptance is overwhelming."

"You'll find our love and family can sometimes be overwhelming, but you're one of us now, Jilly."

"Thank you."

As the chords of the organ began the age-old tune, Stratton escorted Jilly down the aisle. Smiles and grins met her, making her feel one with the community, one with the world.

Jeff waited near the altar, standing next to Russell. His gaze snagged hers, drawing her near. The love in his eyes spoke volumes.

As Stratton reached the front pew, he handed her to the man who would soon be her husband. The man who was her very best friend.

Jilly took Jeff's arm and joined him in front of the altar. Her heart beat with excitement and fulfillment. This was it. All of her hopes and dreams had fallen into place.

Jeff covered her hand with his and flashed her a smile that promised everything would be all right, now that they were together.

Pastor Rayburn cleared his voice, then began the service that would join Jeff Forsythe and Jilly Davis as man and wife.

"We are gathered together," the minister began, addressing the congregation, their family and friends, "to join this man and this woman in holy wedlock."

Before God and man, Jilly Davis and Jeff Forsythe promised to love each other for all time.

Best friends and lovers forever.

\* \* \* \* \*

## Celebrating
## *Blaze*™ **10** *years of*
## red-hot reads

Featuring a special August author lineup of
six fan-favorite authors who have written
for Blaze™ from the beginning!

---

## The Original Sexy Six:

**Vicki Lewis Thompson**

**Tori Carrington**

**Kimberly Raye**

**Debbi Rawlins**

**Julie Leto**

**Jo Leigh**

---

Pick up all six Blaze™
Special Collectors' Edition titles!

## August 2011

Plus visit
**HarlequinInsideRomance.com**
and click on the Series Excitement Tab
for exclusive Blaze™ 10th Anniversary content!

www.Harlequin.com

**Harlequin®**

# SPECIAL EDITION

### Life, Love, Family and Top Authors!

IN AUGUST, HARLEQUIN SPECIAL EDITION FEATURES
*USA TODAY* BESTSELLING AUTHORS
*MARIE FERRARELLA* AND *ALLISON LEIGH*.

## THE BABY WORE A BADGE
### BY *MARIE FERRARELLA*

The second title in the **Montana Mavericks:
The Texans Are Coming!** miniseries....

Suddenly single father Jake Castro has his hands full with
the baby he never expected—and with a beautiful young
woman too wise for her years.

## COURTNEY'S BABY PLAN
### BY *ALLISON LEIGH*

The third title in the **Return to the Double C** miniseries....

Tired of waiting for Mr. Right, nurse Courtney Clay takes
matters into her own hands to create the family she's
always wanted— but her surly patient may just be
the Mr. Right she's been searching for all along.

---

**Look for these titles and others in August 2011
from Harlequin Special Edition wherever books are sold.**

BIG SKY BRIDE, BE MINE! *(Northridge Nuptials)* by *VICTORIA PADE*
THE MOMMY MIRACLE by *LILIAN DARCY*
THE MOGUL'S MAYBE MARRIAGE by *MINDY KLASKY*
LIAM'S PERFECT WOMAN by *BETH KERY*

---

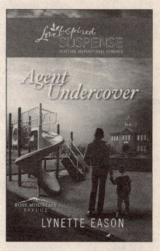

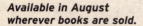